ANASAZI MEDIUM

By

G G Collins

Copyright © 2020 by G G Collins

All rights reserved. No part of this book may be reproduced, distributed, or transmitted in any form or by any means, or stored in a database or retrieval system, without prior written permission from the publisher, except in the case of brief quotations embodied in critical articles and reviews.

This book is a work of fiction. Any references to historical events, real people or real places are used fictitiously. Other names, characters, places, and events are products of the author's imagination, and any resemblance to actual events or places or persons, living or dead, is entirely coincidental.

Chamisa Canyon Publishing
chamisacanyon@live.com
Attn: Rights & Permissions

Book Cover & Interior by Vila Design
Editing by Jay Terre

ISBN 978-1-7354282-0-8
ISBN 978-0-9884674-3-9 (eBook)

Books by G G Collins

Rachel Blackstone Paranormal Mysteries

Reluctant Medium

Lemurian Medium

Atomic Medium

Anasazi Medium

Presence: A Rachel Blackstone Paranormal Mystery Short Story

Taylor Browning Cozy Mysteries

Dead Editor File

Looking Glass Editor

Murder USA: A Crime Fiction Tour of the Nation (anthology, contributor)

(Teen & YA)

Flying Change

Without Notice

Forthcoming

Editor Kill Fee

Skinwalker Medium

Author's Note

Beautiful Bandelier National Monument is New Mexico True. Visit it yourself and learn the wonders of the Ancient Puebloans. It's like walking back in time. If you're feeling up to the challenge, climb the ladders to the Alcove House. It will take your breath away.

Valles Caldera, a dormant supervolcano, is located west of Los Alamos and the LANL (Los Alamos National Laboratory). Featured in the *Longmire* TV series as the sheriff's ranch, it is even more spectacular in person.

For this story, I have adapted the end of the Hopi Fourth World and fictionalized it. The Hopi are Native Americans who live primarily in Arizona. Known as the peaceful people, they have many rich and sacred traditions.

Acknowledgements & Gratitude

Although writing is a solitary occupation, it is not accomplished in a vacuum.

My thanks to MJT for her assistance with my character's crystal education and her abiding encouragement.

And to my husband who reads and rereads my drafts. He's also a damn fine brainstormer.

For MJ

Ami, muse, praticien de cristal.

When all the trees have been cut down,
When all the animals have been hunted,
When all the waters are polluted,
When all the air is unsafe to breathe,
Only then will you discover you cannot eat money ...

– Cree Prophecy

CHAPTER 1

The computer screen went black; followed immediately by her desk lamp. It wasn't yet dark in Santa Fe, but the sun was on its way down.

"Dammit, not again," Rachel swore. The City Different was known to lose power from time to time so while not yet concerned, she was frustrated by the outage.

"It should be called The City Dark. Hey, we're on deadline!" She nodded to her tortie cat, Chile Pod.

But Chile Pod was in alert mode; ears pricked forward, green eyes wide, colorful neck scruff raised.

"What? What is it?"

Before she could sort it out, a wolf howled. It carried across the city, both eerie and urgent. Rachel had heard it before; Kiyiya, the spirit wolf who always seemed to be around when she needed a heads-up.

Rachel really didn't want to get up and look outside. It would be so much better to continue to sit in her kitchen corner safe in her ignorance. She reluctantly pushed her chair back and stood. Before she could cross the kitchen, her house shuddered. Things—a lot of things—began hitting the roof and sides of the house. This was no ordinary hailstorm, an occurrence fairly common to this southwestern city. They must be huge stones. Usually, Santa Fe received small hailstones that tended to go *splut* when they impacted. This sounded more like rocks striking.

When a window shattered, she ducked.

"Chile, get under the ... !" But the tiny cat was already under the table perched on a chair peeking from beneath the stripes of the brightly colored tablecloth.

Rachel raised her eyes upward although there was nothing to see but her ceiling. No explanation was forthcoming. As she reached the window something dark hit the pane, cracked it, and bounced off. She stared in horror at what was happening in her backyard.

"This can't be!" she cried, holding both hands over her mouth.

But it was. Birds were falling from the sky, hundreds of them.

Sensing there was nothing dangerous inside, Chile Pod jumped to the counter to see for herself. Rachel covered her protectively as she watched the ghastly precipitation event. In a few seconds, they abruptly stopped falling.

"Stay inside please," Rachel said to Chile Pod. "I don't want to have to worry about you too."

The storm door creaked as she pushed it open and cautiously stepped outside. There were birds lying on her stoop. She grabbed the broom next to the door and carefully moved them to one side so she could go down the steps. They all appeared to be dead. Rachel had read about this phenomenon. It was normally caused by loud noises such as fireworks that caused disorientation or a flock flew into a hailstorm and died of blunt force trauma. Of course, doomsday predictors had a lot to say about such events and what they felt was the impending Armageddon.

Rachel was wiping tears as she walked carefully through the bird kill. She found it incredibly sad. Once she had navigated the stone path to the courtyard terrace continuing to use the broom to make a path in the midst of so many bodies, she stopped to observe the sunset. It was another spectacular display of colors stretching across a limitless sky, completely unaware of the tragedy that lay upon the ground.

A lone bird righted itself and stood unsteadily. It fluffed its wing feathers as if conducting a pre-flight inspection. None of the others moved. He would have a lonely journey.

Rachel surveyed the bird kill with trepidation and gloom. What had caused uninjured birds to fall from the sky? When the power returned, she would check the internet for similar incidents.

Her attention was quickly captured as cold air closed in around her. Within seconds, she could see her breath. It gathered in a white cloud and slowly drifted away. She held the broom handle in one hand, clutching her arms about her. It felt like winter had come too soon. Rachel was certain that something frightening was about to happen. She was learning the signs: the wolf howl equaled bizarre episodes. She waited. It wasn't her show, but she wished whoever or whatever would get on with it.

She became aware of a sound, low at first; a familiar rattle. It reminded her of the first time she had witnessed the return of a spirit in her Tulsa living room only last year when she attempted to return her dead father for a chat. It didn't go well. Rachel waited; helpless to hasten a ghost making a return voyage, perhaps from a much earlier time.

Streams of fog appeared from four directions, crossing her courtyard with excruciating sluggishness. Oddly, each vaporous rivulet carried a different tint: black, white, red and yellow. Native Americans believed these represented the four colors of humankind as well as the four directions. When the colors united, a figure began to take shape.

The rattling stopped as the vapor integrated and became one in the center of her flagstone terrace.

Rachel stood quietly, hardly daring to breathe, every muscle taut with readiness. Just because she'd experienced this before didn't mean she was immune to fear.

A body was fashioned in front of her. This person was wearing little. She saw a great deal of skin. And a spear! Of course she had no weapon unless a broom constituted one. Just how did one prepare for any eventuality? Ray gun for alien beings? AK-47 for homegrown terrorists? Stardust for pissed off fairies? These occurrences were potluck affairs.

A Native American man walked out of the mist. He was very fit, not the fitness that comes from working out in a gym, but from physical toil. This was someone who labored outside. He wore a simple loincloth, made from an animal skin and shoes made of the same that reached to his knees.

His presence was disturbing. It wasn't just the spear, but she perceived him as warrior. This was someone to be feared. Rachel watched him carefully, reminding herself he was in spirit, but also aware that spirits could cause great harm, even kill. She was ready to run, not that it would do much good.

He stepped toward her, shoes soundless on the stones.

"You are the one?" he asked. He spoke in a language she had never heard, but the words appeared in English in her mind, her own kind of closed captioning.

"I don't know," she replied not knowing if he understood. "Who are you looking for?"

"The one who speaks with the dead."

"I believe I'm speaking with a spirit now. Is that true? Are you in spirit?"

"I am from the Land of the Dead."

"How can I help you?"

She wished she'd stayed near her back door instead of backing into a corner. When would she learn to have these unscheduled meetings on her terms? Could they happen on her terms?

"All the signs except one have been fulfilled," he said. "You must stop the last one or the world will end and another begins. This will not be good. All will die."

"What? What sign?"

"The ninth sign is near to completion. It must be stopped."

"What has to be stopped?" Rachel needed more information. She was even more apprehensive about this man's prediction than his formidable stature and spike.

"The ninth sign. A Blue Kachina in the sky. If it occurs, the Fourth World will end, all will die. The Fifth World will commence, but without all living creatures."

She remembered an interview a few years ago with the Hopi shaman Joseph. He had mentioned these signs.

Rachel could feel the urgency in his words, but didn't understand.

"It is the blue star; the brightest in the night sky," he explained.

"The Dog Star; Sirius?" she asked.

"Yes."

"Are you speaking of the Hopi legend?" she asked.

"It is not legend," he said. "It will happen."

"What will happen to it?" she asked.

"If bad men are not stopped, the star will fall to the Earth and destroy the Fourth World."

"Bad men? That could be almost anyone, anyplace."

"These men will kill our land, our valley where we lived in stone walls."

"But, what can I do?"

"You have the power of the writing instrument. You must expose them."

"And if I can't?"

"Everyone you know and everyone you do not know will die. You will die. Your feline will die."

Had he seen Chile Pod in the kitchen window? How did he know?

"Can you give me more information? I don't know where to start."

He turned and pointed north. "In our ancestral lands," he said and faded away.

The mist dispersed and the cold evaporated on a breeze. But Rachel felt chilled to the bone.

CHAPTER 2

She walked carefully through the bodies of creatures as old as the dinosaurs, went inside, checked on Chile Pod and answered the phone.

"Rachel," it was Chloe. "What the hell is going on? There are dead birds all over the city!"

"And naturally you thought of me?"

"Well?" Chloe prompted.

"I know. I just had a visit. Let's meet and talk."

An hour later, Rachel had lovingly picked up the dead birds, said a blessing over their bodies and made arrangements to have the window glass replaced. She tacked a few mismatched boards over the shattered glass. It would have to do for now.

While she had been disposing of the bird bodies including those in her drive and the street directly in front of her house, she noticed her neighbors out doing the same. One woman was crying and crossing herself as she lovingly picked up birds and placed them in a sack.

Santa Fe is not rich with street sweepers, but one was working the street down the block probably on the way to the Roundhouse so state legislators wouldn't have to cope with the carnage. There were a few advantages to living in her South Capitol neighborhood.

The sweeper pushed them to the side while refuge workers and homeowners bagged them. It was a heartbreaking sight. Rachel felt like crying too.

Once the way was cleared, she backed out the Merc and headed downtown. Shop owners were cleaning sidewalks and helping with the streets. Rachel parked on a street already cleared of avian remains and hoofed it carefully the rest of the way.

When she arrived at The Shed, Chloe was sitting at the bar, margaritas in hand. Everyone was talking about the bird kill. From scraps of conversation she could hear, most were horrified, but drinking was coaxing away the revulsion. A few, like Rachel, had donned gloves and picked up the poor creatures themselves while others were awaiting sanitation crews who made their living cleaning up life's ugliness.

Tomorrow she would call Lloyd Loretto to come smudge her backyard. He was a local shaman who also worked on her car. Her new garage had just been finished and he could clear it too. It was nice to finally have a garage that attached to her house for safety—and the big Merc would fit inside after it was cleansed by her favorite shaman. He would be come soon to work his magic.

This evening Chloe's hair was swept up in an elegant knot. Two Spanish combs held it in place. Chloe was always a stunner and tonight was no exception in a black skinny jumpsuit and blood red ornate cape. Rachel suspected some of the stones on the fabric were not rhinestones. Her friend rarely talked money, but she was loaded what with having the most successful real estate business in Santa Fe and coming from a wealthy French family who sent her on educational cruises for summer break when she was a kid.

By contrast, even with her raise as editor, Rachel's income was considerably more modest. But Chloe always maintained that Rachel's job was far more interesting than hers.

"Tell me about this visit," Chloe said. "I know it wasn't of this earth so just get on to the good stuff."

Rachel related the conversation she had with the ancient Native American and his dire predictions for the human and animal population if bad men could not be stopped from destroying his ancestral home nearby.

"How nearby?" Chloe asked.

"I can't be sure, but he pointed north said they lived in stone walls. There are plenty of sites nearby that are located within canyon walls."

"And he was from the Land of the Dead?" Chloe asked.

"That is what he said," Rachel replied sipping her drink.

"I remember Joseph telling me the Hopi believe the spirit leaves the body on the fourth day after death. Therefore, the body must be prepared properly and buried before then. After burial, a stick is inserted into the grave for the soul to escape to the afterworld."

"And that is how he can travel here?"

"Can't answer that," Rachel said thoughtfully.

"What did he mean by the Fourth World coming to an end?"

"Apparently, we are living in the Fourth World," Rachel said. "If these men, whoever they are succeed at whatever they are doing, we are all doomed. He said the Dog Star will fall and wipe out all life on our little planet."

"A dinosaur apocalypse," Chloe mused. "So now, all we have to do is figure out who these men are and what they are planning."

"Yes, that's all," Rachel said sarcastically.

"Years ago when I did the first interview with Joseph at the Hopi reservation he told me there were nine signs to be fulfilled. At the time I equated it to the end times that Christianity predicts. He said that was an accurate comparison and a new world would appear afterward."

"And did he say which sign we were currently in?" Chloe asked.

"Yes," Rachel swallowed. "The ninth."

"Oh," Chloe said. "That's scary. And on that note, maybe we should adjourn."

As they walked east along Palace under the long blue portal they were quietly reflective. Rachel's rubber soles made no sound on the bricks while Chloe's heels clicked rhythmically.

Rachel stopped and looked up at the heavens. "See there," she pointed to the southern sky. "That is the Dog Star."

“The blue one?” Chloe asked.

“Yes, the bright blue star, straight down from Orion’s belt.”

“I can’t remember seeing that star so large before,” Chloe said.

“You’re right. It never has been. And this time of year it is normally beneath the horizon and not visible to us at all. ”

“It’s like a comet with no tail, heading right for planet Earth,” Chloe commented and then sucked in her breath. “Rachel, we have to solve this quickly.”

They stood in the darkness, the only two people looking up at the sky. Others hurried by on their way to dinner, theatre or one last stroll of the Santa Fe Plaza. All blissfully unaware of what was brewing in the sky.

Rachel cleared her throat. “With all due haste.”

CHAPTER 3

When Rachel arrived at the office the following morning Stella was waiting for her with a handful of messages and a bright "good morning."

Stella Dallas was the office manager, and yes, her mother had been a Barbara Stanwyck fan. But Stella never seemed to tire of telling people how she came by her name.

"When you get upstairs," she added. "Jules wants a quick word."

"Okay," Rachel said and bounded up the stairs. She passed by her office and walked down the second-floor open walkway to Julian's.

"Rachel Blackstone reporting in," she saluted.

"Oh good lord, humor is out of character for you this early," he said.

"Guess I'm just glad to be alive."

"I hear that," Jules said. "Does the bird kill have anything to do with you?" He raised one bushy grey eyebrow. "Should I expect my senior writer and new editor to disappear again for a few days?"

"Yes, I did receive a visit which occurred after the poor birds fell, but thus far I really don't know what I'm dealing with. Chloe and I may have to research some of the nearby cliff dwellings."

"Hope you're not planning an overnight," Jules said. "Somehow, I can't see Chloe as the camping type."

"That could be interesting all right; although, she'd likely have it catered and the food would be good, if inappropriate, for the outdoor experience."

Jules laughed. He knew Chloe and her expensive tastes.

"No MREs for her!" she said.

"Come in, take a seat, I've a new story to run by you. You always get first choice."

"I'm all ears."

"Interesting that you should mention cliff dwellings," Jules said. "Bandelier National Monument was established a century ago this last year. A number of New Mexico publications did stories on our national parks and monuments. I want to add our two cents on Bandelier. Would you like to write it?"

"Oh yes! I'll definitely take that one."

"Okay," Jules crunched his bearded chin with his hand. "Sounds like serendipity to me. Get out of here."

"Running to my office like a good little reporter," Rachel said as she disappeared out the open door.

Once inside her office, Rachel stood at the window that looked out at the Sangre de Cristo Mountains. It was early autumn and just a few of the aspen were turning yellow. In a few weeks the mountainside would be gold and green; a beautiful season in Santa Fe.

Jules had gotten her a "new" desk, in that it was used but in very good shape. She no longer had a Steelcase desk like the poor grunts downstairs, but a beautiful light-stained pine with the New Mexico sun logo on the front panel. A matching credenza held her landline and printer. Inside a drawer was her laptop. Yes, *High Desert Country* had gone big time.

Mari-Lynn, by way of Chloe, had sent crystals with instructions to protect her office. She had carefully followed Mari-Lynn's directions to place one black tourmaline and one selenite stone in each corner. Mari-Lynn said to think of black tourmaline as a guardian angel and selenite as a potent self-charging crystal. Together the stones made for a powerful protection amalgamation. She had used the ends of the large window sill for two sets; a lovely pot she bought from a Native American vendor at the Palace of the Governors guarded the third corner. It rested on top of a small table. The fourth corner had been challenging, behind the door.

With limited sewing skills, Rachel had attached the remaining stones to a small wind chime and hung it from a hinge. It made a tranquil sound when opened and always reminded her that she was cared for.

She pulled out the laptop and depressed the start key; time for some research. The press kit Jules had given her on Bandelier was glossy and factual, but likely wouldn't go into the depth she needed for the story—or more mystical research.

CHAPTER 4

The next morning Rachel was on her way to Bandelier. She passed the exit for the open air opera house and a few minutes later Camel Rock and the namesake casino across the highway. As always when she drove through the Española Valley it took her breath away. It spread both ways from the highway serving up a pallet of pink and tan rock formations accented by green shrubs. It was flat out beautiful. She knew that the famous Cerro Pedernal, or just Pedernal to locals, was in the distance. Its name was Spanish for "flint hill" and had been a favorite subject of artist Georgia O'Keeffe.

She executed the exchange near Pojoaque, drove by the famous Otowi Bridge she and Chloe navigated one frightening night during a supernatural trip back to the Manhattan Project. This time, she bypassed Los Alamos and headed for Bandelier. The landscape became more beautiful the closer she got to her destination changing from wide open vistas with sheer cliffs falling away from the highway to a narrow paved road intimately enclosed with rock formations and desert flora. Once she was through the thoroughly modern town of White Rock, the last segment of the trip went downhill into Frijoles Canyon, one of the highlights of the Bandelier Monument.

Once at the park, the entrance fee was waived since she was there on assignment. She absently looked at the book titles displayed in the visitor center while she waited. Rachel wanted a couple of the books on the national monument for background.

"Hi, are you Ms. Blackstone? I'm Dave Chee, ranger here at Bandelier."

He held out an ample hand and Rachel shook it. Chee was tall, about six feet Rachel guessed, dark hair with some silver creeping in his sideburns, deep brown eyes and an easy smile. She couldn't help but like the first impression.

"Yes," she said. "Please call me Rachel.

"Are you Navajo?" she added, thinking Chee was a Navajo name.

"Yes, my family has lived on the res in Arizona for generations. I moved here when a park service opportunity became available. As much as I love my native land, northern New Mexico became my new home and I've been walking Bandelier's ancient pathways since.

"Speaking of walking, I see you're wearing hiking boots. I was told you want to see the Alcove House, what we used to call the Ceremonial Cave?"

"Yes, please. I'm familiar with the Main Loop, but it's been a long time since I've been any further from the visitors' center."

The Main Loop encompasses the cliff dwellings once occupied by much earlier residents. It's a gentle mile if you are okay with steps.

"Then you know it's about a mile hike followed by climbing?"

"Oh yes. I'm game."

"Had a TV crew out here recently," Chee said. "They were a little surprised we didn't have transportation other than our feet; hiked more than two miles hefting that equipment.

"Let's go. It's a nice day in the canyon."

Rachel started her recorder, opened her notebook, placing it on top of the recorder for a better writing surface. Over time she had discovered small tricks that made doing an interview outside easier.

They took a left and crossed the wooden bridge. It had the feel of magic with golden cottonwoods creating a beautiful canopy over it. Leaves the color of sunlight dusted the foot boards beneath her feet. Autumn was well underway in

Bandelier. She pocketed her recorder for a second, turned and took a photo with the office camera. If she didn't capture it now, she'd regret missing the moment.

Across the canyon were the well-known cliff dwellings, some quite high, in the walls of Frijoles Canyon. Some morning visitors to the park were climbing the ladders put out by the Park Service for a look inside the cavates, or caves, carved from the stone. Children loved to crawl inside and pretend they were people of the cliffs. Many adults couldn't resist a look inside either. Rachel was one of them.

They passed the circular ruins of Tyuonyi. The pueblo structures dated between 1150 to 1300 CE. They had once formed a central plaza several stories high. With time and abandonment it had fallen in, the fragments of the roof beams rested in an ancient jumble of clay dust and shards on the lowest floor. With only one opening to the east, Tyuonyi was once a fortress. At its apex, the community boasted 400 rooms or more and three kivas.

As she gazed upon the rubble from a far earlier period, it suddenly came to life. Rachel blinked, sure she had imagined it. But it was still there and people were going about their daily lives. Women were crafting pottery, men drying hides and families were tending small gardens of corn, squash and beans. Originally the seeds had been a gift from the Great Spirit.

The plants seemed to grow in the earth in square sections surrounded by tiny levies. Mothers and daughters cooked over open fires. Kids played about the many ladders that led to the domiciles. She wanted to walk over and see it all up close, but was startled by ranger Chee.

"You okay Rachel?" he asked.

"What? Yes."

"Did the Ancestral Puebloans grow crops in the canyon?" Rachel used the term preferred by the Pueblo Natives of New Mexico. The word Anasazi is a Navajo word meaning "enemy of my ancestors." The Hopi find it insulting and reject the term Anasazi preferring Hisatsinom or Ancient Ones. There remain deep-seated animosities between the Hopi and the Navajo over land and boundaries.

"Well yes, some. Most of their food was grown on the mesas because the canyon walls block the sun for long periods during the day. But they did grow small gardens here near home; mostly corn, beans and squash that they called the 'Three Sisters' or 'Our Sustainers.' Corn and beans together make a complete protein."

"And did they make small dirt walls around their plants?"

"I see you've been reading our website," he smiled.

"Yeah. Right." Yes she had, but not about this.

"As you know New Mexico is the most water-challenged state. Water was and is at a premium so they formed small barriers around their plantings to help hold in precious moisture. They also used pumice, which is prevalent here from past volcanic activity in the Jemez, as mulch because it holds water and releases it slowly; really quite resourceful.

"You sure you're alright," he asked. "I thought for a moment the sun was getting you."

"Oh yes. Thanks. I was just imaging how it must have been for the ancient ones.

"I understand you have a program to get kids involved?" she switched subjects.

"Yes," Chee replied. "It was part of our Centennial Initiative we created. It's called No Child in New Mexico Left Inside. We want area children as well as visitors to have a feeling of investment in great parks and monuments like Bandelier. It will not only enrich their lives, but help ensure these treasures will endure long after we're gone. And we want kids to be outside exploring and having fun."

"I assume the curriculum is age-specific?" Rachel asked.

"Yes. Kids can become junior rangers. It's also an environmental outreach program that transports students and teachers to the park and provides training and teaching tools for instructors.

"Another aspect of that initiative was the renovation of the Visitor Center. While we updated things like electrical, removed asbestos from our heating system and improved accessibility, we also took down non-historical walls and added original windows long hidden in some closet. You've seen the new bookstore."

The two had been walking along, and sometimes crossing Frijoles Creek along the way.

"Well, here we are," Chee said.

"That seemed like a quick walk," Rachel exclaimed. Then she saw the sign at the base of the trail and that old familiar knot in her stomach returned.

The notice on the sign described the ascent as 140 feet. It went on to suggest that people with health problems or fear of heights should not partake. Children should be supervised. Climbing was limited to ladders; no off trail excitement here. Rachel thought the trail more than exciting enough as it was.

Rachel remembered her father bringing her here when she was a child. She was so excited, but soon wanted to go home. The climb was achieved through a series of paths, stone steps and long ladders. Although the ladders are quite sturdy and there are landings between climbing sections, it is an exciting adventure to the top. Rachel wondered if her will was up to date.

The first ladder wasn't scary and somewhat protected on both sides by earth, but as they continued along the path and steps, carved from the stone canyon wall and guarded by a rail, Rachel began to feel very exposed and high. But the next ladder was tall with nothing to stop her from falling. Fortunately, it was angled so it wasn't a straight-up climb. It topped out at a landing and another ladder, which was far scarier. Rachel tried not to look down but instead concentrate on placing each foot on the rungs. This one seemed more vertical. She kept telling herself: one foot after the other. No reason you can't do this. The next landing didn't have a protective railing and she gasped at the canyon below. But there was one more ladder, a shorter one, and then some remaining steps to arrive at the top.

When they finally reached the Alcove House, they caught their breath. While the effort wasn't difficult physically—not counting fear of heights—the elevation of more than 6500 feet added to the exertion.

"It's just as beautiful as I remember," Rachel said. The golden cottonwoods almost divided the canyon along the stream below. Their foliage was in stark contrast to the tall ponderosa pine and the mixed green conifers above them.

"We believe about 25 people lived in this dwelling. The kiva was reconstructed due to age and disrepair," Chee said. "They had quite a view."

"Okay if I go inside the kiva?"

"Yes, please do."

She descended a short ladder into the underground room. Kivas were used as ceremonial chambers and sometimes included fires. Rachel could feel the spiritual energy within the earthen room. How many souls had visited? How many prayers had been carried away on a breeze? When she scaled the ladder, the sun made her blink back the brightness. Rachel scanned the other side of Frijoles Canyon, the timberline of ponderosa pine, the unforgiving cliffs, and the flat mesa where the ancestral Pueblo people cultivated their crops. It was at once intimidating and beautiful.

As she imagined what their day-to-day lives must have been like, the scene seemed to swim. At first, she thought she must be feeling the effects of vertigo, but she stood straight and tall, despite the way the cave floor sloped away to the edge of the cliff.

The images that came into view were not of the canyon but of a river or arroyo. The water running between its banks was not of normal color. It was yellow-orange. People lined the river covering their mouths with whatever they had; their hands, clothing. The surface of the water became clear. Now she knew why they were so repulsed. Dead fish floated everywhere. Something was dreadfully wrong.

She closed her eyes for a moment to stop the vision, but when she reopened them there was movement across the canyon to the west. It was too far to make it out, but whatever it was, it was out of place.

"Rachel. Hello. You still here?" Chee said.

"Yes," she said. "Just admiring the view. Say, can you see movement on the western mesa?"

Chee took out binoculars and scanned the cliffs.

"All I see is dust. Could you tell what it was?" he asked.

"No, I guess it was nothing."

She snapped several photos with the office camera. "That should do it."

"Ready to go back?"

"Yes, lets."

When they were a short distance from the visitor center, Chee stopped her.

"You know, when my mother's face looks the way yours did earlier, she has visions, especially in places like this," he said. "Here's my card. It has my cell on it. If you need to, call me."

"Visions huh?" she muttered, not wanting to admit that.

"She tells me it's a gift," he said.

"How long did it take for her to think of it like that?" Rachel wanted to make sure she wasn't being set up for a putdown, but intuitively felt Chee was on the level.

He smiled. "A while," he admitted.

Rachel accepted his card and thanked him for his time. It included his email so she could thank him, something she always tried to do after an interview. Busy people took time from their work day to talk with her. The least she could do was thank them.

All the way back to the office all she could think about was yellow water and dead fish.

CHAPTER 5

Later as she poured out food for Chile Pod in her kitchen, a story on the news caught her attention. It was accompanied by film of space focused on a blue star. The female anchor wearing the latest coif, read from the teleprompter:

Scientists can't explain why Sirius, the Dog Star, seems to be slowly approaching Earth. But calculations have in fact shown it is closer. No alarms have been raised yet, but careful monitoring is being done by NOAA, NASA and other scientific groups. In the meantime, the star is gathering cautious admirers.

The phone rang the second the story ended.

"Rachel," it was Chloe. "Did you see the story on the Dog Star?"

"Yup. So we aren't the only people keeping an eye on that star."

"Nope."

"How did the hike in Bandelier go?" Chloe asked.

"Okay, but I saw something disturbing while there."

"Disturbing how?"

"Remember when the bumbling EPA inadvertently released million of gallons of heavy metal waste from an old gold mine into the Animas River turning it yellow?" Rachel asked.

"Of course," Chloe said. "It continued downstream and infected the San Juan River too. It was a major clusterfuck."

"Even after the EPA said it was safe, the Navajo Nation declined to use their irrigation canals for one year, as I recall," Rachel said.

"The EPA said it wasn't responsible for damage that might be done to livestock or crops," Chloe said. "Who would ever believe that an agency designed to protect the country from such debacles would actually cause one," Chloe said in disgust. "Course, they don't live here, so what the hell?"

"But they were sorry."

"Uh-huh."

"Do you recall if there were any fish kills?"

"Only a few I think, but fishing was not allowed for some time after. Why do you ask?"

"Because what I saw was yellow water and hundreds of dead fish floating in the river. It must have created a horrible stench as people were covering their mouths and noses with whatever they had."

"You're concerned it will happen again?" Chloe asked.

"Yes. That about covers it."

"Something's going on for sure," Chloe said. "I've got a house to show. I'll check back in with you later." She was gone.

Rachel quickly dialed the phone. "Do you have some time? I'm in need of someone who knows more history than I."

The drive down Agua Fria was more fractious than usual. Two narrow lanes and rush hour was a bad combination. She pulled the big Merc into the drive, thinking about what questions to ask.

F. Dominic Magellan opened the door of his ubiquitous adobe house. His dog Juan was barking madly, scooting all over the floor.

"Does he know he's not a pit bull?" Rachel asked above the ruckus.

"Shush. You'll give him a complex," Dominic pushed his shaggy blonde hair back from his face.

He motioned her in and pulled out a chair from the table. "Can I get you something? I've got water, tea or beer."

"Nothing thanks. I've just got a simple question." She sat but her mind was so busy her body didn't want to be still.

"Uh, Rachel, nothing is ever simple with you. What's going on now? Had any unusual visitors lately?"

"Well, yes, sort of," she hemmed and hawed and gave him the quick version. "What I need to know is about Hopi prophecy, specifically, about the end of the Fourth World as they see it."

He stood and checked his bookshelves, of which there were many. Dominic had been named after the Portuguese explorer. His father left him and his mother after his birth. He didn't care much for his first name. He had a graduate degree in psychology and paid the bills as a corporate trainer and soul navigator. But he also had a Ph.D. in ancient cultures. Dominic helped Rachel when a Mayan man-eating deity became a threat. She trusted and liked him.

He quickly chose a book. Thumbing through it, he found what he wanted.

"There are nine signs in all. They range from the white man taking their lands to a variety of forecasts such as covered wagons, longhorn cattle, railroads, power lines or the World Wide Web, highways and the long hair hippies of the 1960s. They believe all have been fulfilled but the last sign."

"Which is?"

"They believe a blue star will appear in the heavens and collide with Earth. When it does that will end the Fourth World and the next will begin. Some have speculated it is the International Space Station because it is reputed that the star is a dwelling place, but of course there is nothing to substantiate that.

"Does this have anything to do with the ever growing presence of Sirius in the night sky?"

"I'm afraid it may," Rachel said.

"Well then, should I be on the lookout for more falling birds?"

"Bad as that is, I'm afraid it could get worse before—or if—it gets better." She gave him the condensed version of what the Hopi spirit had told her.

When she returned home, Rachel did a search of her own on her computer. She needed to fact-check what Dominic had told her. Website after website about the Hopi confirmed every detail that she had learned from Dominic.

The gist was this:

The First Sign: White-skinned people who took land and struck with thunder. Thunder was interpreted to be guns.

The Second Sign: Spinning wheels filled with voices. This was thought to be covered wagons coming west occupied with settlers.

The Third Sign: A beast similar to a buffalo but with great long horns will arrive in large numbers; such as longhorn cattle.

The Fourth Sign: The land will be crossed by snakes of iron; railroad tracks.

The Fifth Sign: Land crisscrossed by a giant spider's web. This could be power and telephone lines or even the World Wide Web.

The Sixth Sign: Rivers of stone that make pictures in the sun. Certainly concrete highways and their mirage-producing effects could explain this sign.

The Seventh Sign: The Sea will turn black, and many living things will die. Could it be oil spills in the Earth's oceans?

The Eighth Sign: Youth who wear their hair long like our people and join the tribal nations to learn our ways and wisdom. Were they hippies? They wore their hair long and some lived in communes following the traditional ways.

The Ninth and Last Sign: A dwelling-place in the heavens shall fall with a great crash. It will appear as a blue star. After this, the ceremonies of the Hopi people will cease.

As would all life according to the Hopi spirit who had visited her.

She absently patted Chile Pod who rested in her lap napping contentedly, certain her guardian had everything in hand. Rachel picked her up and held Chile more for her own comfort.

But from the cold spot in her stomach, Rachel was certain that something awful was coming she didn't know how to stop it. And stop what? Where did the evil men come in and who were they?

The phone rang.

"Hi Rach, it's me." Chloe said. "I'm turning onto your street. Are you busy?"

"No, in fact, I'd like to share something with you."

Rachel printed off the information on the Nine Signs of the

Hopi. She popped a couple of Negra Modelos and they sat down at her table. Chloe read the list.

"Holy shit," she said. "Is this what we're dealing with?"

"Yes, I think so."

"But that would mean ..." Chloe lifted a finely arched brow.

"All the signs have been fulfilled but one."

They picked up their bottles and walked into Rachel's courtyard. Dusk settled in around them; the end of another day. Usually Rachel enjoyed evening. Tonight it was full of foreboding.

"There it is," Chloe pointed. The Dog Star was bigger and bluer than ever.

CHAPTER 6

Rachel woke to what she thought were the first strands of light finding their way through her curtains. Disoriented, at first she didn't know if it was a dream or real. The sound seemed to come from all around her. It rumbled as if a train was going by, but Rachel's house was so far from the Rail Runner station that she never heard it. It wasn't the Emergency Management siren because it wailed and this didn't sound like it at all.

But the light in the room wasn't from the rising sun, but from the white wolf Kiyiya; Rachel's spirit wolf and protector. He stood at the foot of her bed growling softly, body glowing white, blue eyes imploring her to take action. He didn't usually make a personal appearance unless the situation warranted it.

"What is it Kiyiya? What's happening?" Rachel asked. She saw the words in her mind: Take Cover. Then his mission completed, he disappeared.

Her visit to Lemuria came flooding back. Her journey to save Stella from the Dracs who kidnapped her, coincided with the demise of the Pacific continent that brought them both within seconds of dying. She had been caught in one of their earthquakes and it had sounded similar to this.

Seconds later, Santa Fe shook. Rachel launched out of bed, but her feet didn't feel steady. The ground undulated beneath her house. It felt as if a giant serpent was tunneling its way below her. Balance was impossible.

She grabbed Chile Pod from the bed and walked unsteadily into the bathroom where the plaster walls were reinforced with tile and there was less ceiling to fall in on them. She opened the linen closet and sat down on the floor leaning over Chile Pod to protect her from falling shampoo bottles and bars of soap. They waited. The seconds ticked by. It was more powerful than the quakes Santa Fe usually had. It wasn't the "big one," but it was giving it a go. Something fell in another room with a crash of breaking glass, but the house held together. Although it seemed much longer, it was over in about a minute. She thought it would never stop. When it finally did, she heard the eerie sound of sifting plaster inside the walls.

Rachel carried Chile Pod with her as she inspected their home. The only casualty was a glass trinket, while having sentimental value, it wasn't a great loss. It had been a gift from her grandmother, a glass bell she bought for Rachel while traveling. She carefully swept it up to prevent any fragments from remaining where Chile Pod could walk on them. Reluctantly, she dumped them into the trash.

"We have to learn to let go, don't we?" She felt a little sad, but didn't have time to pursue it.

Rachel placed Chile Pod in a chair and went to check the gas water heater. It seemed okay, no movement, but she would look into having it strapped to the wall. She'd read that water heaters could *walk* during an earthquake. Oh, the things she'd learned covering every imaginable topic as a staff reporter.

The phone rang.

"Hello Chloe."

"How did you know it was me?"

"I do have caller ID and well, it just figured. Did you have any losses at your house?"

"A couple pots fell from a shelf. Nothing I can't replace," Chloe said. "Do you know anything about this?"

"Other than it was an earthquake. No."

"Why don't you gather the Pod and come over for breakfast?"

"Are we having waffles?"

"That could be arranged." Rachel thought she could hear Chloe scoff.

* * *

Fifteen minutes later, Rachel turned the Merc off Gonzales onto Chloe's *dirt* road. For some inexplicable reason, a dirt road—actually gravel, and never graded—was a prized possession in Santa Fe. That way, your car stayed fashionably dusty. Luxury cars were common but they had to be dirty. Rachel thought there must be an unwritten law to that effect. The piñon, although slow growing, was again infringing on the car space and scratching the Merc's navy sides.

"Shit. I guess we'll have to bring the loppers next time," she said to Chile Pod who was immersed in her new world out the car window. The pet safety seat was carefully seat-belted for her protection; a gift from Auntie Chloe.

Rachel parked and walked through Chloe's herb bed to the back door.

"Come in, come in," Chloe greeted them. "The waffles are on the way and I have a new treat for the little Pod Girl."

"That I'm sure I can't afford," Rachel said, but knew it would be in vain.

"It will be her treat when she visits Auntie Chloe."

Apparently, it was quite luscious as the Pod lapped it up in a couple bites, and then jumped on the banco surrounding the kitchen table and curled up on a cushion.

"Well, I guess a two-mile car ride is tiring for a cat," Rachel sighed.

"More likely the earthquake," Chloe said thoughtfully. "I can't remember an earthquake more recently than about 2011? 2012?"

"It was 2011," Rachel said. "We did a story on earthquakes in the Santa Fe area. There were two that year, but they are infrequent even though we have a moderate chance of them. Some occur that can't be felt."

"Look," Chloe pointed to her flat screen and turned up the volume.

"We made national," Rachel said. "And since when do you watch news?"

"I fear your incessant news watching is rubbing off on me," Chloe retorted.

This morning New Mexico residents awoke to a whole lot of shaking. An earthquake of 5.6 in strength rocked the Land of Enchantment. There was some minor damage, but no injuries or deaths have been reported. It's unclear what may have caused the tremor.

"That's way bigger than the 3.0 or less we usually get," Rachel said. "That's worrisome. What could be causing a quake that powerful?"

The doorbell rang and Chloe scooted out of the room, returning with a large white sack. She removed recyclable boxes and opened them on the table.

"Here are your waffles," Chloe smiled a sweet but reprimanding grin, crossing her arms for effect.

"Where's the syrup?" Rachel looked at the luscious looking waffles with no syrup.

"I think the caterer meant you to have this fruit with your waffle," Chloe pushed the container of fruit next to her plate.

"Fruit?" Rachel asked. "As in no syrup?"

"You know chile is a fruit?" Chloe said. "You eat it in large quantities."

"Yup. So I get plenty of fruit." Rachel refused to get pulled into another discussion on digestive health. "I'll make you a deal. I'll eat the berries with syrup."

Chloe gave up and retrieved a bottle of pure maple syrup from her cabinets.

"There," she said. "Knock yourself out. At least it's the real thing and you'll get vitamins and minerals from it."

"Okay, good." Rachel acknowledged, dousing the waffles in the sweet amber liquid. She didn't look, but knew Chloe would be frowning, so she ate the blueberries in two gulps.

Rachel pulled a piece of paper from a pocket in her bag, unfolded it and gave it to Chloe.

"I did more research on the end of the Fourth World of the Hopi. What do you think?"

Chloe thoughtfully read it.

"The signs seem straightforward and the explanations as to their fulfillment do seem point-on. But I'm not sure about the ninth one. The only dwelling place in the sky—that we know of—is the space station. That doesn't explain the Dog Star growing in size every day. And, there's nothing here about earthquakes."

"Yeah, I thought of that too. Of course, the quake might not be related; could be coincidental."

"But do you believe in coincidence anymore?" Chloe asked.

"Not so much. Maybe I should do some research into what could be causing a quake in a city that rarely has them."

"With everything going on, that's a very good idea. Can I help?"

"Yes. Chloe, can you check for building permits, things along the real estate line?"

"Of course."

"I'll check other records, like dam construction, drilling or roads. These are things that might use earth movers, explosives or other heavy equipment."

"Rachel, I do think it's imperative we move quickly."

"Yes, I have that same sense."

"Uh, Rach," Chloe said. "I've got to tell you something. You're probably going to be upset."

"Thanks. Like there isn't enough to upset me already. Out with it," Rachel replied.

"I think I saw Chris earlier today."

"As in my brother Chris?" Rachel asked.

"Yes. Did you have any idea he was being released from prison?"

"No," Rachel said. "It's not something I've kept up with. You can do that, but I haven't."

"You might want to check it out. I would swear I saw him coming out of the county mining permits office," Chloe added. "Why would he go there?"

Chris Woods was Santa Fe's mayor at the time Rachel returned to the city. Their relationship had been strained since their father's death. Chris had gotten involved with bad sorts. They turned on him. He was kidnapped, nearly killed and then sent to prison for his part in a real estate scam. Rachel hadn't really thought about what it would be like seeing him again, or if she even wanted to.

"I've no idea," Rachel said. "But it better be for a job interview and not some new nefarious activity."

"Sorry to be the bearer of bad news," Chloe said.

"Better I hear it from you," Rachel replied. "Right now, I prefer not to run into him."

CHAPTER 7

The office was all abuzz about the quake.

"Felt like a freight train crawling under my house," Shorty said, *High Desert Country's* photographer. At one time he had intimate knowledge of the workings of the aging copy machine, but due to the renovations that Jules had done, the office now had a state-of-the-art copy machine. The only problem was the staff wasn't state-of-the-art, leading to frequent cries emanating from the new copy and supply room.

"Scared the shit out of me," Moon said. "I was flat on the floor under the table with my dog and a pillow. Thought it would never end; maybe we would die. My apartment is on the second floor and it was swaying. Had I eaten, I would have tossed my cookies."

Rachel sprinted up the steps to her office not wanting to hear anymore. It had been bad enough without adding her coworkers' experiences. Once her computer desktop appeared she starting searching for information. First, she typed in vinelink.com. It was used to determine if an offender had been released from the prison population. She selected the state, typed in Chris Woods name and waited. And there it was: he was out.

Her whole body went rigid. Chris was out. What could that mean? Anything? Nothing? But it was there in black and white.

It didn't imply her life had to change. Maybe he would never contact her; maybe they would never talk again. She had tried to visit him in prison a couple of times, but he always refused. Rachel gave up.

There were more important things to be concerned about right now. She tried to put this revelation out of her mind and focus on the earthquake.

Returning to her computer she cleared her history and checked on earthquake frequency in Santa Fe finding only three tremors since 1931 within 30 miles; all under 3.5 on the Richter scale.

She found that during a 2014 study of the Raton Basin done by the Seismological Society of America that “ongoing seismicity in the Raton basin” was found to be caused by “deep injection of wastewater from the coal-bed methane field is responsible for inducing the majority of seismicity since 2001.” It had also been linked to contamination of drinking water in Colorado.

Much like Oklahoma whose state government ignored all the science and warnings and continued to use injection wells, or fracking, until there were two large quakes of 5.6 and 5.8, felt from Texas to Indiana; only then did they begin to seriously shut down wells. But they only decommissioned the wells in the areas where the quakes were most prevalent and violent. The idea was to “control” the quakes not to stop them. Because of this practice, Oklahoma became the state with the most earthquakes in the lower forty-eight, going from two in 2008 to nearly 900 in 2015, becoming three times more likely to experience earthquakes than California. Was New Mexico experiencing the same thing?

Drilling was definitely something she needed to check on. She took a quick look at the oil and gas production in New Mexico and found no permits had been issued close enough to Santa Fe to cause harm. Rachel hoped that wasn’t a dead end.

She went on to check on possible dam building, road construction and mining. Still nothing similar that would require explosives. It was the only thing Rachel could think of that would cause faults to slip other than fracking. New Mexico had more than 4500 such wells. And they wouldn’t necessarily have to be close by to cause seismic activity hundreds of miles away.

It appeared an impossible question to answer. She tried looking at a map of New Mexico depicting its drilling and mining sites.

What if it was a water issue? She located a map of the state's aquifers. There she learned that Peabody Coal had used billions of gallons of water during the years of 1965 to 2004 from the Hopi and Navajo aquifers to the extent of nearly emptying out the underground reservoir. It also provided power and water for personal use for people living in Arizona, Nevada and California. As a result, some Indian tribes still didn't have running water or electricity on their reservations. This had led to cries of environmental racism.

As of April 2016, 38 percent of people living on the Navajo rez did not have running water necessitating long trips to fill containers and haul water back to their homes. Many still used outhouses because they limited their water usage to 10 gallons a day, while boomtowns of the southwest used 100 to 200 gallons per day per person. The Bellagio Hotel fountain in Las Vegas wasted 12,000 gallons per year to evaporation.

On Hopi lands, they too were having issues with water. Those who had modern plumbing discovered the water had twice the arsenic level the EPA said was safe. Was any arsenic safe? It wasn't until the 1980s when running water came to the rez that the Hopi people began to report it tasted odd. While two new deeper wells were drilled, the tribe needed millions more dollars to complete the project. Meanwhile, the cancer risk was intolerable.

How situations like this continued over decades in supposedly the richest country on the planet? If the Star Ancestors were inflicting punishment via the Dog Star, you really couldn't blame them.

Rachel was more confused than ever. There were many things evil men could do that could cause seismic activity, polluted water and dead birds. How could she make sense of it in time to prevent Chloe's dinosaur apocalypse?

She looked at the maps again weighing the options for destruction. In a millisecond, she was overwhelmed with horror. Staring her in the face all along was something she had completely forgotten about: the New Mexico supervolcano!

CHAPTER 8

"University of New Mexico. How may I direct your call?"

"Rachel Blackstone with *High Desert Country* magazine. I need to schedule an interview with the geology department regarding the recent earthquake."

"I'll ring media relations."

"Media relations; this is Carrie."

Rachel ran through her spiel again. Carrie placed her on hold while she called to see who was available.

"Putting you through," Carrie was gone.

"Earth and Planetary Science," the receptionist said.

"I'm Rachel ... "

"Oh yes, I'm expecting you. I'll get Professor Saxon on the line for you."

"Ms. Blackstone? I'm Axel Saxon. How can I help?"

"I'm senior reporter with *High Desert Country*. We're concerned about the recent earthquake and how it might affect the Valles Caldera supervolcano. Would it be possible to talk with you in person?" Face-to-face interviews were almost always better than a phoner because she had visual clues to observe. This could appear in the form of facial, hand and body movements. Often she could tell if someone was lying and had learned to confirm flat-footed statements.

"I have a free period this afternoon. Would two o'clock work for you?"

"I'll be there. Thank you."

Later that day, Rachel took "The 25" at St. Francis and headed the Merc south to the Duke City. Although Albuquerque is a mile-high city like Denver, its moniker came from Don Francisco Cuervo y Valdez, who was the provisional governor of the territory. But where does the Duke come in?

Valdez petitioned the then Spanish government to change the name to Alburquerque, after Viceroy Francisco Fernandez de la Cueva, the Duke of Alburquerque (the 8th one). Some prominent person at the time couldn't pronounce Alburquerque, because of that pesky first "r" so it was dropped and the nickname shortened to the "Duke City."

There is also a story about the name coming from John Wayne who received his nickname while working on a film about the 19th Duke of Alburquerque. It involved a dog and a baseball team and was so convoluted Rachel preferred the other narrative.

She took the exit for Central Avenue, Albuquerque's piece of Route 66. Shortly she crossed University, and a few blocks later took a left at Yale. Northrop Hall was near parking. She found a visitor spot and slipped her press vehicle ID onto the dash. She refused to stick it to the window. On some assignments it's better not to let people know who you are for security reasons or just as an element of surprise, but today she thought it prudent. No towing charges for the Merc. She clipped her personal press pass to her jacket pocket and entered academia.

Universities were odd places full of rules and traditions that were nearly as complicated as they were immovable. Even in journalism college she'd found it a stifling environment. Reporting was such a free flowing occupation in many ways. She liked to think of herself as on a lengthy bungee cord; as long as she made deadline, Julian didn't care when or where she did her work. It was a job that allowed her to be outside a lot. Rachel enjoyed walking beneath the turquoise sky that usually covered New Mexico. The high dry climate agreed with her and it was heaven to be out in it and not closed up in an office all day.

"Are you Rachel Blackstone?" She had found Saxon office and his assistant greeted her.

"Guilty."

"Dr. Saxon is ready to talk with you."

Saxon was just short of six feet tall. His hair was mostly black, while his goatee was silver. Those piercing dark brown eyes were likely menacing to young students.

"How do you do? I'm Rachel Blackstone." She held out her hand.

He took it. Nice firm handshake.

"Please sit down. How can I help you?"

Rachel placed the old-fashioned recorder on his desk and took out a notebook. As a person without a cell phone, she saw no need to update her recorder either. No digital for her, just tiny cassette tapes.

"We're concerned the earthquake we had yesterday could have some dire effect on the Valles Caldera west of Los Alamos National Labs and Bandelier. Obviously the LANL produces plutonium and has a nuclear materials storage facility that is rumored to have been built over faults." The LANL is the site of the original Atomic City built by the Manhattan Project. The project produced the first bomb created by splitting an atom. The ghastly result ended WWII.

"I'm also doing coverage on Bandelier and this has caused some question as to its future. Obviously, the issues with Los Alamos Labs and a volcano going off right next to it are of grave concern."

"We too are troubled by the earthquake, particularly its intensity," he said. "Currently, we do not know what caused it, but the epicenter was approximately here." He pushed a map toward her and placed a pen on the spot. It was west of Bandelier. "We've checked and no drilling or mining permits have been issued there. We simply don't know what caused it yet."

"How dangerous is the Valles Caldera?" Rachel asked.

"It is considered a young supervolcano in that it erupted 1.25 million years ago. It's geothermal and responsible for the hot springs that populate the area. We also know it is dormant, not extinct. The caldera is about 20 kilometres or 13 miles wide. A supervolcano isn't one eruption, but multiple eruptions occurring at once. When the volcanic pressure cooker just can't take anymore and it releases pent up energy in many places." He showed Rachel another map showing the resurgent lava dome, called Redondo Peak, and the smaller domes around it.

"If it were to erupt again," Rachel asked. "What force are we talking about?"

"Supervolcanoes have an eruption of magnitude eight," Saxon paused. "That's the largest on the VEI or Volcanic Explosivity Index."

"So this type of eruption really isn't within our experience in the near past?" Rachel asked.

"No. You've heard of Pinatubo, Krakatau and a U.S. volcano called Mount St. Helens?"

Rachel nodded.

"These are inconsequential by comparison to the Valles Caldera. Even Crater Lake and Tambora are smaller. Only the Yellowstone supervolcano is larger. Are you aware that the last time the Yellowstone erupted that ash and dead animal bones were found as far away as Nebraska? The three Yellowstone eruptions we know about produced enough ash to fill the Grand Canyon and were 2500 times larger than the 1980 eruption of Mount St. Helens. Today, if Yellowstone went off it would immediately kill 90,000 people. Those not dead would be standing calf-deep in ash. The nuclear winter to follow could cause famine as the great breadbasket of the world, the States, would likely not be able to grow much."

"What would the results be of a Valles Caldera eruption?" Rachel asked.

"First there would be the ash fallout to consider. Not only would any planes in the area be at risk of losing engine performance and therefore crash, but water contamination could result and rooftop collapse. That is especially a problem for flat roofs that can be found all over our area, but especially prominent in Santa Fe due to the Pueblo architecture.

"Agriculture would be adversely affected, maybe not even possible. Livestock would become ill and die from breathing the ash and gases.

"People would also experience health issues and some, maybe many, would die. It would depend on the size of the eruption.

"We don't even know how it would affect power-producing plants. And yes, we don't know if the damage to the LANL would be sufficient to release plutonium and other nuclear materials into the air. If so, that could be cataclysmic in terms of loss of life.

"As to the influence on the country and the world; again, depending on the size of eruption, it could bring about the nuclear winter where ash would block the sun and make agriculture impossible. And this brings me to the most lasting product of supervolcanoes: worldwide famine, millions—maybe billions—of refugees, satellite disruption and the crash of world financial markets."

"Good god," Rachel said. "All because a New Mexico volcano wakes up." She was quiet a moment.

"I'm afraid so," Saxon said. "We would be on our own."

"My last question," she said. "Could drilling or explosives use set off the Valles Caldera?"

He rubbed his chin thoughtfully, weighing what he was about to say. Rachel waited.

"I would have to say it's possible. Whatever is going on at that epicenter needs to cease. We have a crew of grad students going out there tomorrow with monitoring equipment. We hope to know more then. I'll email you the findings.

Rachel thanked him.

As she left the geology building by the side door, she wondered if someone was watching her. She donned her sunglasses so she could glance about inconspicuously. Rachel opened her tablet and pretended to check her notes. Looking around, there were several people walking about, hurrying to class or an appointment. And then, without turning her head, she saw a man standing behind a sprawling chamisa. There was something familiar about him, but she couldn't be certain from this distance. She snapped her notebook closed and returned to her car.

The trip home was sobering. Rachel wondered about aftershocks and how large they might be. When she returned to her office she checked the USGS website and found that aftershocks had already occurred, but she hadn't felt them in Santa Fe. Most had been in the 2.0 to 3.0 size. That might have felt like a small ripple or wave, unnoticeable in a car or walking around. But a supervolcano was truly frightening to think about. No one in the immediate area would live if it roared back to life. Not Rachel or anyone; just as the spiritual visitor told her.

CHAPTER 9

It was deadline day; Rachel finished fact-checking and editing her stories that were due. She put her computer away in the desk drawer and locked it. Time to go; Lloyd Loretto the shaman was coming by to sage her new garage.

When Rachel pulled into her driveway, Lloyd was right behind her. The tall Native American man carried a large abalone shell she recognized from when he cleansed her house.

"Hello Lloyd," she said. "How are you today?"

"The Great Spirit has been kind to me today. And you?"

"Kind of a disconcerting day, but I'm well."

He nodded as if he understood. Maybe he did.

Rachel opened the garage door with her remote. Her car remained outside in the drive.

Lloyd lit the white sage, the most powerful of the sage plants, and allowed it to burn for a few moments before blowing out the flame. He now had good smoke. First he cleaned his hands with the smolder and then permitted it to touch his face and chest to cleanse his mind and heart. He began on the left side of the doorway, using a feather to waft the smoke from the sage against all the walls and into the corners.

In turn, he lit and fanned burning sweetgrass for good spirits and followed with Native American grown tobacco to lift the prayer to the Creator.

He spoke softly in his native language. While Rachel didn't understand it, she knew he was praying for any negative spirits to exit the dwelling and inviting good spirits in. When he had smudged each wall and stood at the entrance, he pushed the remaining smoke from the garage where he lifted the shell and ashes upward to each of the four directions. When finished, he placed the ashes on the driveway in front of the door.

"Your auto casa is purified," Lloyd said, making reference to the repair garage where he worked: Juan's Auto Casa. Juan and his brother had rescued her one scary night in the countryside west of Santa Fe. They had towed and repaired her car. She had sworn right then to never go elsewhere. It was a comfort that they employed Lloyd who decontaminated vehicles on request. With Rachel's extracurricular activities, knowing a shaman was useful.

"I'll go cleanse your courtyard now," Lloyd said. "Why does it need it?"

Rachel thought a moment and said, "Because of the bird kill. I want their spirits to fly freely."

"Why do you hesitate? Is there something more?" Lloyd was intuitive.

"There may have been a spiritual encounter too."

He nodded and disappeared for a few minutes. When he returned he said, "Do not worry. The birds are flying into the heavens. And the spirit you spoke with means no harm."

Rachel was astonished. How did he know?

"I spoke with him," Lloyd said as if he had read her thoughts.

"That's a relief. Thank you," Rachel said and shook Lloyd's hand. He was a shy man and she was afraid a hug would be too much, but she was fond of him. He slowly walked back to his pickup; he was never in a hurry, each moment was to be savored. His work was done.

Rachel stepped inside the garage and breathed in a little of the residual smoke to cleanse herself. The garage hadn't been used yet. She wanted to wait until Lloyd had worked his magic. The garage door closed with the squeeze of her remote and she went inside the house to check on Chile Pod who had watched the ceremony from the living room window.

The phone was ringing as she entered the front door.

"Rachel if you don't get a cell phone, I'm going to get you a GPS watch." It was Chloe.

"¿Qué pasa?"

"Have you heard the latest?" Chloe asked.

"What latest?"

"A team from UNM sent to investigate the epicenter of the quake didn't return."

"What! How can that be? They know the area like the back of their collective hand."

"A search party is being sent, but it's so late in the day, they likely can't find them this evening."

"I think I'll go to Bandelier in the morning and see if anything or anyone turns up," Rachel said.

"Not without me!" Chloe returned.

"Uh, Chloe, this would require a sleeping bag, no bathroom facilities and MREs for dinner. Are you sure?"

"Of course. I've been camping before."

"But that was a luxury safari where you had real beds in really, really nice tents, all your food was prepared for you and your stuff was driven to the next stop."

"Close enough," Chloe said with confidence. "Only no MREs. I'll bring the food. I'm sure the caterer can fix a picnic that will be trail worthy."

"Okay," Rachel said cautiously. "There won't be refrigeration either and no one to carry our backpacks."

"How about an ice chest?"

"Oh no, that wouldn't work because we'd have to carry it. We need things that we can cool in a stream, like beer and cheese."

"Consider it done. I'll throw in some fruit. We'll dine lavishly."

That's what I'm afraid of, Rachel thought.

"I'll pick you up in my partner's SUV," Chloe said. "It will be much better than the Merc, as you so lovingly call the gas guzzling bus you drive."

"That might hurt its feelings," Rachel said. "But Lloyd saged the garage today so it can spend its first night in the new auto casa."

"I'll be by mid-morning then," Chloe said.

Rachel hung up and looked at Chile Pod.

"Auntie Chloe's going camping." She could swear the cat raised an eyebrow.

CHAPTER 10

The next day, Chloe knocked on the door.

"I've got Chile Pod settled in with plenty of food and water," Rachel said. She grabbed a small backpack with a sleeping bag, bug spray, TP, water and yes, some MREs just in case they were needed. "Dominic is going to check in on her too."

"Have you set your alarm?" Chloe asked.

"Oh shit. I wish I hadn't had it installed; such a hassle. And you know, it doesn't alert for spiritual visits. I still need the Pod and Kiyiya for that."

"But it's worth it to protect the Pod girl."

Rachel had to admit she was right. Chile Pod was her family now; with her father dead and her brother in the state pen. Of course, Chloe, Dominic, Julian, Stella and the rest of the *High Desert Country* staff were all extended family. She was loved and appreciated; couldn't ask for more.

Rachel eyed the large backpack in the truck with suspicion.

"Are you sure you can carry that?"

"Yes," Chloe said. "It's not that heavy."

"Ooh-kay," Rachel said, doubt written on her brow.

On the way to Bandelier, Rachel related her visit to UNM and what she had learned about the Valles Caldera.

"So even a baby supervolcano is larger, stronger and more dangerous than Tambora in the early 1800s that caused climate cooling, crop failures and produced the year without a summer," Chloe marveled.

"Yup," Rachel said. "And all we have to do is stop it from happening."

"How do we keep getting into these dilemmas?"Chloe asked.

"Because I decided one night to try to return my father from the dead for a talk," Rachel said. "Big mistake."

"The biggest, but can't change that now."

They stopped by Bandelier to pick up backcountry permits. Rachel gave the approximate location where they would camp and left names and numbers of friends should they go missing.

"Which way?" Chloe asked back behind the steering wheel.

"Highway four. Once we reach Forest Road 289, it will take us to the trailhead."

"Which trail are we hiking?" Chloe asked.

"The Alamo Boundary Trail," Rachel said. "It's easy and kid-friendly so I thought you could do it, what with you packing the kitchen sink.

Chloe glowered.

"This trail also acts as the boundary between Bandelier and the Valles Caldera."

"How much elevation do we gain?" Chloe asked.

"About 400 feet."

Chloe made the turn off the highway onto the Dome Road, so called because it leads to St. Peters Dome. The dome was the highest of several 8,000-foot peaks and includes a watch tower. The main purpose is to scout for forest fires. Access is only by foot.

"How far?"

"A few miles," Rachel said. "The trail begins in the Santa Fe National Forest and we crossover into Bandelier."

It was a rough several miles, but not as frightening as traversing the creaking one-lane Otowi Bridge to Los Alamos' Atomic City during the 1940s in their last adventure.

Shortly, Chloe reached the trailhead and parked the SUV setting the brake.

Chloe retrieved her backpack and heaved it onto her shoulders.

"Do you think you can walk a mile and change with that?"

"Sure."

But Rachel wasn't at all sure. She set off at an easy pace.

"At least you wore sensible shoes," Rachel observed. "No heels. They look expensive."

"I bought them yesterday at REI," Chloe said.

"You mean they're not broken in?"

"The salesman, who was very cute, told me if the shoes fit correctly you don't have to break them in."

"Okay," Rachel said. "You do get an 'A' for footwear this time."

"Why Rachel, I thought I'd never hear those words."

Rachel pursed her lips and gave Chloe the look. Chloe just laughed. She let no one get to her.

They began walking toward Bandelier through the forest. It wasn't a tough hike, and it was lovely where the wildfires hadn't touched the land.

"Looks like we're it," Chloe said after about 30 minutes. "Haven't seen person or animal."

"This looks like a good place to stop." Rachel dropped her backpack on the ground near a small grove of trees.

"Do you need help with the tent?" Chloe asked.

"Uh no. Didn't bring one."

"No tent? Sleeping bags only?"

"Yup. *Au naturel*. Well, almost."

"What about wild animals?" Chloe asked. "Won't we be vulnerable?"

"If you want to build a shelter; I won't stop you," Rachel said a little annoyed.

"Okay, sleeping bags only," Chloe said with a sheepish look. "How about some food? She began emptying out her backpack until at least a dozen small boxes littered the ground. Rachel observed Chloe's payload would be much lighter on the return trip.

An hour later having gorged on delicacies that had likely never before been consumed in the wild, Rachel took the remaining food, stashed it in a bag and then hung it in a tree for safekeeping. A nearby stream kept the bottled water chilled.

"Are there facilities?" Chloe asked.

"As in a flushing toilet?" Rachel inquired.

"I was hoping for something other than the ground."

"What you see is what you get." Rachel waved a hand around their small-forested area.

"Okay." Chloe heaved herself from the fallen tree where she had dined. "It's off into the unknown."

"Don't rub against anything with three leaves," Rachel cautioned, snickering a little tossing her a roll of TP. Chloe caught it.

"And this." Rachel handed her a small camping trowel.

"Uh, gee thanks Rachel, but I'm only going to pee."

"To bury the toilet paper," Rachel said.

"Oh. Okay." Chloe walked away stopping behind some chamisa.

She looked around and couldn't see anyone for miles. Shit, she thought, I could actually be caught with my pants down. That's why people invented plumbing.

Chloe tried to balance on both feet without tipping backward. The squat was awkward even though that was how people had evolved in the first place. Finally, with all systems go, she produced a stream that hit the ground and splashed a bit. She adjusted for it and everything was proceeding normally. That is until the puddle reached her shoes.

For a few minutes, Rachel enjoyed the tranquility of the outdoors. It was a quiet like nothing else, and yet it was filled with life. She was shaken from her musings when Chloe shrieked. Rachel jumped up and headed toward the sound.

"It's okay," Chloe shouted. "I forgot to squat uphill so as not to get pee on my shoes."

Rachel laughed and headed back to her perch. She was still chuckling when Chloe returned.

"Did you ruin those expensive new hikers?" she sputtered.

"Like you care," Chloe tried to regain her dignity.

"Bound to step in something unsavory eventually."

"You always find the positive in everything Rachel," Chloe said with thinly veiled sarcasm.

Rachel grinned. She was beginning to feel sleepy; full stomach and a blanket of stars to contemplate. But it was short-lived. Looking at the sky had reminded her of the Dog Star. She walked a few paces away from the trees and gazed up at the vast galaxy.

"Chloe, come look."

"Do you suppose people watched Halley's Comet every night?" Chloe asked.

"I once read that some people sold their possessions because they believed the world was about to end," Rachel said. "They would gather together and watch it in amazement and horror."

"I get the horror part," Chloe said.

"Shall we get some sleep?"

"Seriously, do you think we'll actually sleep out here? I thought this was more of a slumber party thing. You know, talk all night."

"If you want to talk all night, do it quietly, I'm sleeping." Rachel said.

"How do we do this?" Chloe asked, struggling with her sleeping bag.

"Unzip the side of the bag and crawl in." Chloe picked hers up off the ground and shook it vigorously.

"There's nothing in it," Rachel said impatiently as she tucked herself in.

"Just being safe."

"Okay, you be safe and I'll be asleep."

CHAPTER 11

Rachel tried to pull out of a heavy sleep. Had she heard something or was she dreaming? No, that was definitely a twig snapping. She sat up. Whoever it was made no attempt to walk quietly.

"Rachel," Chloe whispered. She scooted her sleeping bag nearer.

"Shush. Let them go by." How she wished they had set up camp deeper in the forest instead of just off the trail.

In the darkness, lit only by the moon, flashlight beams bounced around the rough country.

"They'll see us," Chloe whispered.

The two women stayed very still and quiet. But when one of the beams found them there was no hiding.

"What do we have here?" One man said crossly.

"We're camping!" Chloe retorted.

"Not here," he said. "This is private property."

"No, it isn't," Rachel said evenly. "This is Bandelier. We signed in with the monument office. They approved it.

The men stood quietly a few moments. Rachel tried to size them up in the dark. They had the advantage. She couldn't see them; they remained behind the dancing lights. They looked like tall men. One was heavy. The thinner man, who hadn't said a word, stepped back almost as if he wanted to stay out of sight. Rachel shook off her sleeping bag and got up. Chloe followed. Standing would offer them a small advantage versus being on the ground. Fortunately they were fully clothed, albeit, shoeless. Standing made Rachel feel less vulnerable.

“Maybe they came all the way out here hoping to party,” the man said. Rachel could practically hear the leer.

Rachel slipped her hand into her pants pocket to double check that the pepper spray was there. It was. She always carried it. It might stop one, but she doubted she have a second opportunity.

“There’s no party going on here. Just a couple of women waiting on their husbands to return from fishing,” she lied. She knew it was feeble and they likely didn’t believe her, but she had to try something.

“Why would they be fishing in the middle of the night?”

“Because they’re idiot men,” Chloe said. “Why are you two out hiking at night?”

“Like I said, you’re on private property. You need to pack up and leave.”

“We’re in Bandelier,” Rachel said again with rancor. “And the Bandelier office knows we’re here.”

Rachel hoped her assertion that people knew where they were was sinking in. This could go bad, fast.

“C’mon,” mumbled the man who couldn’t be seen. There was something familiar about his voice, but Rachel was too preoccupied with the situation to consider what that was.

“You’ve been warned,” the heavy guy said. “If you don’t listen, we’re not responsible.” A veiled threat?

“If you know what’s good for you,” the other said. “You’ll get the hell out in a hurry. No second warning.”

With that, they turned and walked away.

“Holy shit,” Chloe let out the breath she must have been holding throughout the encounter.

“I’ll say. Let’s get our shoes on and move our stuff into the trees, off the path.”

When everything was out of sight, Rachel said, “Let’s go see what they’re up to.”

“You mean, follow them?” Chloe’s voice was full of doubt.

“They have a head start. They won’t hear us. We’ll keep a safe distance.”

"Oh sure. Why not? I wasn't planning on living much longer anyway, what with the Dog Star obliterating planet Earth at any moment."

"Maybe we can uncover what's going on," Rachel said. "They didn't have backpacks, just torches and they're wandering around out here. Obviously they didn't expect to run into anyone."

"Yeah. Hiking at night makes about as much sense as fishing," Chloe grumbled."

"Let your eyes get adjusted to the dark. We'll take a flash, but only turn it on if absolutely necessary. If they look back, they could see the light."

"Oh geez Rachel, did you have this in mind when you thought of this excursion?"

"No, but we have an opportunity, expected or not."

"Then let's go," Chloe sighed. "It may be the only break we get."

* * *

After at least thirty minutes of stumbling in the limited natural light, they saw a small slice of light in the distance.

"Rachel, we need to be careful. Those guys are bound to be here."

"Yup, let's get off the trail and see if we can come at it from another direction."

They crept through trees trying to be as quiet as possible. Despite their efforts, the occasional twig snapped alerting the wildlife to take flight. The trees gave way to a clearing.

"I hate to ask Rachel, but should we get down on all fours?"

"Yeah. I can see the light again over that berm."

By the time they reached the raised ground, they were crawling. Carefully, they looked over the side. Below them was a valley with a thick covering of trees. The light they had noticed before suddenly disappeared leaving the night lit only by the moon and stars.

"Do you hear that?" Chloe said.

"Yeah, a vehicle is coming."

As they watched, a truck appeared. It wasn't using its headlights. Only split seconds of red reflections.

"What the hell? Why would anyone be driving without lights?"

"We may be about to find out," Rachel said.

The truck came to a stop and waited, motor running. A man said something indistinct. Moments later, the earth opened and a dim light filled the void. Almost immediately, it was blocked out by the truck. And then, poof, the vehicle was swallowed whole.

CHAPTER 12

"What the ... !" Rachel said under her breath fearing she would be heard in the absolute quiet that followed the vanishing.

"What is going on?" Chloe whispered.

"I haven't a clue. But judging from how fast that happened, it is suspicious at the very least."

"Could you tell what kind of truck it was?" Chloe asked. "I thought it might be a tanker."

"If you're right, what are they transporting?" Rachel said. "Tankers carry gasoline, oil, liquefied gas, even milk. Of course, fuel can explode. That could explain the earthquake, but if one of the tankers had exploded, surely they wouldn't still be working here."

"Could be more than once site," Chloe offered.

"Let's go back before we get caught. We might actually get a couple of hours sleep."

They crawled to the woods where they watched the puzzling scene in the middle of nowhere; Rachel thought she saw the sliver of light appear again. A shadow moved through it and it disappeared.

"Do you think that was another truck?" Chloe asked.

"I wasn't even sure I saw anything, but it did look as if something went through one way or the other," Rachel replied. "It's difficult to see even close up because the truck was nearly obscured by that mound near the opening."

Chloe thought a moment. "What is going on?"

"Don't ask me," Rachel said. "I'm certain those men would be angry if they caught us here. Let's go back."

The return trip was easier since they were now familiar with the trail, still there were slips and near falls in the darkness. When they reached their campsite, they spread their sleeping bags beneath piñon trees next to a grove of ponderosa pine so as not to be sitting ducks if another night visitor walked past.

"This feels safer," Chloe whispered as she brushed her hair.

"I agree. We're completely surrounded by vegetation," Rachel whispered back. "Difficult to see the sky, but I'm more than ready for sleep. As long as we don't turn on any lights, we should be fine until dawn."

"That isn't far away." Chloe looked around them and seemed satisfied they were secure. She pushed her body into the bed roll and zipped it up.

"What, you're not going to shake it out this time?" Rachel kidded.

"I'm more worried by who's out there than what might be in my sleeping bag."

Rachel followed suit and they slept for several hours until the sun began to part the morning clouds and created the colors artists from around the world come to paint. They packed up their belongings and headed east.

"Let's take this trail," Rachel said. "And try to stay away from the one we took last night. I don't like the idea of meeting those guys again."

"Nor do I," Chloe agreed. "Or explaining what mindless thing our *husbands* are doing this morning." They both snickered.

A good twenty minutes later, Rachel stopped abruptly.

"Hey," Chloe said plowing into her. "Your brake lights aren't working."

"Sorry. Uh Chloe, that looks out of place." Rachel pointed ahead. The open path was about to end. Ahead was a wall of rock where the trail led. Not somewhere that Rachel wanted to go, but she was afraid they had found what was missing.

"Looks like a pile of trash was left behind. Aren't people supposed to pack that out?"

"Yes," Rachel said absently. "But I think I see an arm."

"What? Someone is napping?" It's difficult for the human brain to accept death where it shouldn't be. Rachel knew her friend was blocking the information she was seeing.

"There's no need for us both to look," Rachel said. "I'll do it."

"No, I'm right behind you." Only Chloe was next to her.

They hesitantly walked toward what looked like bodies, only to find two men who were beyond help. Their bodies lay in a heap of twisted arms and legs, faces covered in bruises. One was wearing a University of New Mexico T-shirt. There were no backpacks or equipment in sight. Surely, they had brought equipment with them.

"Oh god, this is awful. They're dead aren't they?"

"Chloe, I'm afraid these are the grad students from UNM sent to check on the seismic activity."

Rachel quickly checked each for a pulse knowing full well it was useless. Their faces were ashen and their eyes stared glassily. Their skin felt cool and unnatural. There was no one to save.

"I'll call for help," Chloe said taking out her phone.

"If there is cell service," Rachel said. "Usually there isn't until you get out of Bandelier and on the way to White Rock or Los Alamos."

Chloe held up the phone as if the sky would respond to her wishes.

"Nothing."

"Do you mind taking photos of the men and the surroundings?" Rachel asked. "That way it will be easier for the rangers to find them."

"Uh, okay." But Chloe didn't move.

"Here, I'll do it," Rachel said.

"No, it's okay. I can do it."

Chloe began taking pictures of the immediate area and then walked over to the bodies and took several more. It looked like she knew what she was doing.

"That's the saddest thing I've ever done," she said. "Should we cover them with something?"

"No, I think that's not the thing to do. It would disturb what is probably a crime scene."

"Then let's get back to where we have cell service and call for help," Chloe said.

It was a quiet hike back. Both women felt the weight of those who find the deceased. The grief for those who have passed and their families who don't know it yet; and the knowledge that the image of those crumpled bodies will stay forever in their consciousness.

By the time they were within a few miles of Los Alamos, Chloe triumphantly cried that they had cell service. Rachel pulled the car over and reached for the phone.

"I've got the cell number of the ranger I met the other day. I'll let him get the ball rolling."

Chee answered his ring right away.

"This is Chee," he said.

"Hi, this is Rachel Blackstone; the reporter. We spoke the other day."

"Yes, of course, I remember. What's up?"

Rachel told him about the discovery. He knew what to do; likely wasn't his first time."

She returned the phone to Chloe.

"Would you send him those pictures?"

"Sure."

Rachel wheeled the SUV back onto the highway. The drive home was full of troubling thoughts. Rachel had noticed the men's arms and legs looked broken. She thought it a good chance that the men had taken a beating and then been thrown from the cliff above the trail. Without their equipment, it seemed to indicate they had died elsewhere. She was certain it hadn't been an accident.

CHAPTER 13

It was a long trip back. Rachel drove because Chloe made the drive to Bandelier. And it was mostly silent as each woman tried to make sense of what happened.

When they reached to outskirts of Santa Fe Rachel asked, "You want to stop for something to eat?"

"Yes," Chloe said. "But let's get take-out. After what we've seen, I don't want to make small talk right now."

"Okay," Rachel said. "I'll stop by Chopstix." She drove through the wide intersection at Paseo de Peralta and North Guadalupe, pulling into the small parking area.

"I'll get it," Rachel said. "What do you want?"

"Uh, whatever veggies they have," Chloe answered.

Rachel went inside and ordered the super spicy chicken, green beans and mushrooms for herself. She usually had great enthusiasm for the spicy chicken, but today she just wanted to eat. She asked for a veggie dinner for Chloe. Rachel thanked the nice Asian woman who she normally took time to chat with, paid and left.

"Here you go," she placed the white bags on the console. "Can you do the honors?"

"Sure." Chloe took the bags and held them in her lap with the care she would a baby.

Automatically, Rachel drove to her house.

"How do you like the garage?" Chloe asked, trying to talk about something besides bodies and whatever was going on at Bandelier.

"I like that it's attached to the house. And Lloyd cleared it for me; along with the courtyard in back."

"That's good," Chloe said in a voice that Rachel barely recognized.

Chile Pod met them at the door and immediately wanted to be picked up. Rachel did so holding her close. Something about this living, breathing creature who loved her set off the tears. She sat down at the table still holding Chile Pod.

"God, that was horrendous," Rachel wiped at her eyes. It was as if she had to hold it in until they got home. Crying and driving wasn't a good combination.

"Yeah," Chloe added. "Seeing someone dead, especially someone who may have been murdered, is a burden that's going to be hard to carry." She pulled a tissue from her pocket and dabbed at her eyes too.

"Chee sounded nice," Chloe tried.

"Yes, he seemed to be," Rachel set Chile Pod on the chair next to her and pulled two beers from her fridge. Mechanically, she opened the bottles, added plates and silverware to the table. "Do you want a glass?"

"No thanks, I'll drink from the bottle this time." Chloe always drank from a glass; this was tantamount to admitting she was having a blue mood. Chloe never had those either.

They transferred the food to plates, but still didn't eat.

"I'd just drink the beer, but I haven't eaten since morning," Chloe said.

"Yeah, we need food," Rachel replied. "Not just for sustenance, but to do something ordinary."

Rachel took a forkful of chicken and barely felt the burn. Usually it was delicious; today it tasted flat. When they had both eaten a little, they put it away in Rachel's near empty refrigerator and adjourned to the living room for a second beer.

"I better go," Chloe said. "I'll bet you have stories to write."

"I admit it," Rachel said. "I've got one due. Fortunately, the rough draft is done so it's a case of finishing rather than beginning with interview transcription."

"Okay then. I'm off." Chloe hugged Rachel and air-kissed. And then, she picked up Chile Pod and repeated. "Take good care of Rachel, she had a bad day, as did Auntie Chloe."

Rachel worked for about an hour making corrections,

fact-checking and polishing her story. When she was done, she emailed it to Jules. If he had questions, she'd see him tomorrow.

She was about to turn off her computer when she decided to do a little research on the Dog Star.

Many civilizations had attached various meanings to the brightest star in the sky. It was also associated with wolves in addition to dogs. The ancient Greeks thought it heralded the wilting of their crops because of its appearance before summer. Early Egyptians based their calendar on its emergence in the sky. But the Hopi viewed it as some sort of death star. Rachel really hoped the Egyptians were right, but couldn't place any hope in that. She'd need to talk with Dominic again. He was better informed when it came to Native American beliefs.

Discouraged by the events of the day, she shut off her computer. Exhausted, Rachel took a hot shower. She would have preferred a bath, but felt the need to wash off the last two days. A shower seemed most effective.

CHAPTER 14

Mari-Lynn sat cross-legged on a meditation cushion in the middle of her Native American medicine wheel. She'd had it constructed as a gift to herself on her most recent birthday. Her home, outside Pueblo stood near a grove of tall pines. The wheel was in the open between the trees and her house. It was the middle of the afternoon and the sun was just beginning to dip to the western sky.

Rachel met Mari-Lynn through Chloe. Originally, Chloe had a business relationship with Mari-Lynn, who was her pot supplier. Now marijuana was legal in Colorado. Sales had been brisk before and remained steady when she became a legal seller of the weed, much to the chagrin of local law enforcement who had tried to arrest her for illegal sales before the change in law. Mari-Lynn always seemed several steps ahead of them.

But Chloe discovered Mari-Lynn was also a crystal expert. She had studied the Native American use of stones in their ceremonies and traveled to the crystal mines. Over the years she learned to recommend them for a variety of uses. Several crystals had been life saving for Rachel. Blue lace agates had saved her from a powerful Drac and opals got her out of a tight pinch with a fiery Nazi alien. She'd also used transitions stones to get a message through to a dear friend who had passed.

Mari-Lynn's gauzy powder blue pheasant dress billowed gently in the light breeze. The sun warmed her face. Her medicine wheel, basically a circle with a cross through it, was made of granite blocks. The pathways were comprised of sandstone and led the traveler to the center of the wheel. It also allowed access to the four quadrants. These quadrants represented the four cardinal directional colors. Each of these spaces was composed with different color stones. It was a peaceful place to meditate.

A dedicated student of meditation, Mari-Lynn was accustomed to thoughts intruding into her quieted mind. Most of the time, she could redirect them. But this time, something really wanted in. She brushed her long silver hair out of her face. Utilizing a common motion could reset her mind. It was similar to turning up the radio in a car when you wanted a change of thought. She focused on the mountain breeze that gently blew by lifting her hair and ruffling her dress. Next, she went back to her breath. In and out. In and out. It was such a lovely day; she simply wasn't prepared for what filled her mind as the images exploded.

Mari-Lynn pitched backward in revulsion. Her eyes flew open, but it didn't stop the pictures. It looked like water, but it was a sickly yellow and objects bobbed and disappeared in the churning liquid. The objects were of various sizes. She felt as if she was in it. The tumultuous water surrounded her and pulled at her body washing over her. Her hands moved involuntarily as she tried to get out of the rancid liquid.

Mari-Lynn concentrated and her body lifted above the scene playing out in her head. She brushed at her clothing as if to fling the sour drops away.

With extreme concentration, she rose higher. And then, she was really horrified. It was water; ugly, deadly water carrying the dead and near dead. But where was she? Taking a moment to look away from the horror below, she scanned the landscape. She appeared to be in a city with a flooding river.

There were many brown stucco buildings. In the near distance was a cathedral, with unfinished steeples. The adobe structures were unmistakable. This was Santa Fe. The aspen was turning golden on the mountains. It was stunning against the green towering pines. The sky was brilliant turquoise, but it was deceptive because something had gone dreadfully wrong.

Her eyes returned to the scene below. People were running in all directions as the fetid waters escaped the bank of the Santa Fe River, spreading poison and dead fish. But one woman stood on a bridge. She could tell from her posture the woman was weighing a decision. Her head turned back and forth as if looking for a solution or assistance. Her fists clenched. Why wasn't she running too?

Mari-Lynn lowered her position. In another moment she saw what the woman saw. A young child was suspended precariously in the treacherous rolling water, clutching desperately at a Styrofoam cooler, while the water rushed her toward the bridge. The water was so high that the child couldn't pass beneath the bridge. If the child wasn't rescued she would crash into the viaduct.

As Mari-Lynn turned to look at the lone person on the bridge, she stifled the urge to call out. She couldn't—not in a vision. But she did recognize the woman. She was Rachel Blackstone. Rachel's face was spellbound in indecision. Mari-Lynn knew her well enough to know that she was trying to make a split-second decision on how to best rescue the child; if that was even possible. Oh god, she had to warn her.

In a heartbeat, Mari-Lynn was back in her meditation circle, safe, but breathing hard. She stood and ran to her house. She had to call Rachel. There was no time to spare; of that she was certain.

CHAPTER 15

Santiago Lopez had patrolled the Buckman Direct Diversion since 2011 when it was completed. He loved being outside. Depending on the day and the weather, he could be travel the area via truck, 3-wheeler or horseback. Today was a glorious day, like so many of the 300 plus days of sunshine in north-central New Mexico. The saddle leather creaked as his paint horse Diablo walked the familiar trails along the Rio Grande where the Direct Diversion was located.

The BDD was part of the Santa Fe water supply infrastructure where water from the Rio Grande was routed to the city of Santa Fe. The city's water supply was multifaceted, with water coming from snowmelt, wells and the Rio Grande. Precious aquifer water was protected so it had time to replenish and was only used when other sources were endangered.

It all began in the Banco Basin in Colorado west of the Continental Divide. The water traveled 26 miles through a tunnel beneath the Divide and then was pumped 11 miles uphill to the BDD where it was treated.

As a desert city, Santa Fe made the decision to conserve water. From its peak in 1995, the city managed to decrease usage by forty percent. The average American uses 150 gallons of water per day. In Santa Fe, this had been lowered to 102 gallons per person. The effort included replacing 44,000 toilets, hotels could only wash linens for long-term guests every fourth day, restaurants could provide a glass of water only to diners who asked for it and sidewalks could no longer be hosed off.

Lopez received a message on his two-way radio. It crackled as he pulled it from his belt.

"Patrol," the unfamiliar voice from the control room said. "Water release incoming."

The message was not unusual. The releases were confidential and he was always notified when to expect them. But he didn't recognize the voice.

"Patrol to control room. Who's speaking?"

"Don Wilkins," the voice said. "I'm new to BDD. Everyone at lunch. Super in the can. He'll be back in a few minutes."

"Okay," Lopez said. "Open the gate."

More time than normal went by before Lopez heard the warning buzzer. He maneuvered Diablo to the edge of the river and waited for the gate to open.

"Hey," Lopez said into the walkie-talkie. "The gate's not opening. You okay in there?"

"That's affirmative," Wilkins replied. "Learning curve, but I'm getting there."

"Okay." But Lopez wondered what someone that inexperienced was doing in the control room.

Diablo stomped his foot to discourage a few flies around his legs. Lopez waited to see the water coming down the river.

Eventually, the gate slowly opened against the water current and locked in place. The new guy had finally gotten his act together.

Lopez thought once again how lucky he was to have this job. He was outside all day, sunshine on his face, and today with his buddy Diablo. He absently patted the horse on the neck. At that moment, he noticed Diablo's ears perk forward, head up. He stamped his foot again, but this time it was different. This wasn't an attempt to fend off flies. Impatience? Was he ready to move on?

Diablo became restless, his front hooves moving back and forth as if he was in distress or even fearful.

"What is it boy?" Lopez patted him again trying to settle him.

It didn't help. The horse became more agitated. His gaze was very specific. He was looking upstream where the water would be rushing at any moment.

Lopez wasn't one to panic, but the horse was definitely behaving strangely.

And then, he saw what Diablo had sensed for several minutes. The water rushing his way was an awful color. It looked like it was mixed with a lot of yellow dirt. Worse, there were fish bobbing on the surface. Lopez grabbed his walkie-talkie.

"Wilkins! Close the gate! Close the gate! Emergency!"

"What? Did you say close the gate? Thought you wanted it opened?"

"There's something wrong with the water. Close the gate!"

"Oh shit," I forgot where that is. "Let me get the check list."

"Something has compromised the river. Close the gate! We don't have time for on-the-job-training."

"Okay, okay. I'm looking."

"Jesus Christ," Lopez muttered. "You've got to close the gate!"

But it was too late. The jaundiced water was pouring into the BDD headed for the Santa Fe River.

Lopez urged Diablo to run from the water. The horse needed no encouragement. With the reins slack, Lopez gave Diablo his head so he could navigate on his own. The horse dodged trees, limbs on the ground and headed up hill clearing the area just as they heard the water crashing onto the banks. Lopez turned once to look at the rancid water headed to Santa Fe. The gate could not close now because fish had blocked the mechanism. There was nothing he could do. He remembered something his father had told him as a child about yellow water and dead fish being some kind of sign.

CHAPTER 16

Magdalena Cristal covered the picnic table along the Santa Fe River with a bright tablecloth while her husband Tomàs unloaded the basket of food from the small pickup parked in the lot.

"Anna," Magdalena said in Spanish. "Come help me."

The quiet 4-year-old did as she was told and helped smooth the cloth of wrinkles. She had to stand on the bench seat, but as was her way, she always did a good job.

"That's great Anna," her mother said. "Here comes your father with the food."

But Anna had been drawn to the river and was silently staring upstream.

"What's the girl thinking now?" Tomàs said as he placed the basket on the table.

Because their daughter was so quiet, they had taken her to their doctor, but the tests he wanted to run were unaffordable to the young family without health insurance living in the richest country in the world. The doctor thought she might be autistic, but her mother wasn't so sure.

Magdalena looked up to see her daughter pointing to something, but by the time she saw the flash flood her voice of warning was drowned out by the roar of the water. She stood unbelieving while her daughter was picked up from the bench and carried away. Tomàs ran after her, but stopped by the out-of-bounds river.

"Get on the table," he shouted to his wife, but she was running after Anna. Magdalena could swim; her husband could not. She dove into the putrid yellow water filled with dead fish and tried to swim to her child, but it was too late. Anna was no longer in sight. The frantic mother swam to the picnic table where she clung to her husband and prayed for her only child.

"We'll find her," Tomàs tried to reassure her, but he had never been so frightened in his life.

Anna bobbed in the raging river trying not to swallow any water, but finding it difficult to stay afloat. She had taken swimming lessons at the recreation center. Her mother was emphatic that she learned to swim. She was too small to fight the water, so she worked at staying above the violent surface.

As she came around a bend there was an old man with very long white hair holding a cooler. She had seen her mother pack their picnic in one just like it. He seemed to float through the air effortlessly as he made his way to her.

He had a look that Anna was familiar with. Her parents called them her invisible friends, but they were visible to her only with a transparent look that most people didn't have. This man had that look; there, but not there.

"Take this," he said and the cooler seemed to come to her as though commanded. "Hold on tight. There will be a woman to save you down the river. Her name is Rachel. You can trust her. Tell her beware cats-ee-nah. Let the power go through you." Anna wasn't sure she could remember all that but it gave her something to think about as she made another turn in the river clinging to the cooler. She could see a bridge ahead and someone standing on it.

The man's face glowed with love and strength and Anna felt it enter her. She was still scared, but much more assured. She grasped the cooler.

"Thank you," she said, but the man was gone.

* * *

Rachel had finished lunch at home when the phone rang. It was Jules.

"Rachel, glad I caught you," he said.

"Uh-huh."

"Can you cover a short news story for me?"

"Sure."

"I know it's not normally your thing, but we need it fast for our headline blog."

"Fire away," Rachel replied folding back her notebook and scrambling for a pen.

"It's downtown. There's a possible water emergency, but our source wasn't certain what. Something about the river."

"Okay, on my way."

She was about to pick up her bag when she noticed a message waiting on the antiquated answering machine. A familiar voice sounded urgent.

"Rachel, this is Mari-Lynn. I've had a vision you need to know about. Now, my manifestations don't always turn out verbatim, but it involves water. You will be called upon soon. Someone may need to be saved. Stay aware. Courage dear."

"That's strange," Rachel said to Chile Pod. "Jules just assigned a water story. Guess I'll have to see what happens."

She smooched the tortie's head and then rubbed it with her fingers.

"That gets the tickle off."

Rachel had no idea how many times she had done this little show of affection, but she thought Chile Pod enjoyed the ritual.

Rachel went through the unfamiliar doorway from her kitchen to the new garage. What a luxury. She felt more secure with this private entrance. No longer would she have to make sprints to her car with bad guys lurking about. But it wouldn't stop those in spirit.

A few minutes later she parked the Merc on the south side of the Santa Fe River in the largest parking space she could find. The car's carriage groaned as she cranked the wheel hard to back it into the parallel spot.

Rachel headed east checking the trees for thugs. Recently a woman had been held up at gunpoint along the river. She would exercise due diligence.

When she came to a narrow footbridge, she walked to the middle and stopped. The old iron railing had been painted brown, but was fading in the strong sunlight.

As Rachel looked east, she noticed several aspen growing from the riverbank had already turned golden. It was a beautiful sight and she expressed her appreciation to the Universe for the pleasure of living in Santa Fe, muggers aside.

Everything looked normal. The river was nothing but a trickle as it often was unless it was spring snow melt or a flash flood during the summer monsoon. The fact that it was an actual river often stumped visitors more used to large flowing rivers like the Mississippi or Columbia.

She was wondering where the water story was when birds began taking flight from the trees. It was as if every bird along the river was suddenly in a great hurry to fly elsewhere, anywhere. A couple of dogs being walked began to bark. The squirrels scurried from the grass up the many trees that populated the park.

"What the hell?" Rachel heard it coming before she could see it.

Rachel focused upstream as far as the bend. Something was definitely up and it was getting louder. She stood transfixed, waiting for what was to come.

In a flash, the river transformed from a dribble to an undulating quagmire of dangerous fast-moving yellow water. It filled the banks quickly and panicked people were fleeing from both sides of the river.

Rachel was about to follow their lead when she saw something floating among the raging water. There were dead fish; lots of dead fish. She recoiled from the sight of them, something right out of a horror film.

The object that transfixed her was a white box. A child was clinging to the container, desperately trying to hold on, but her head kept disappearing beneath the flood waters.

"Hold on!" Rachel yelled.

It became clear the little girl was fighting exhaustion and her grasp wasn't secure. She was smart; her arm was over the side of the Styrofoam container, the contents having been lost. Beer and soda cans, mixed with the squalid river and its horrific bounty of dead fish moved quickly toward Rachel.

The river was leaving its banks and Rachel could see if the child wasn't rescued, she and the cooler would crash into the side of the bridge where she stood. Frantically, she looked around for someone who could help, but people were running for their lives and only glancing back to assess their immediate threat.

She was alone in this. Battling her instinct to run too, she shouted at the child.

"Grab my hand!" Rachel leaned over the bridge, one hand holding the railing the other hanging down to catch the girl.

"I can't," the girl yelled, obviously terrified.

"You have to. Grab my hand!"

Hesitancy passed over the child's face.

"Let go!" Rachel screamed over the rushing river.

She nodded no.

"Let go! Grab my hand!"

Water was now coming over the bridge.

The frightened girl let go of the cooler. That increased her speed and her fear.

"Hands up!" Rachel shouted.

She was rewarded by the girl's uplifted arms. Anna was within a few feet of the bridge. Terror didn't begin to describe the girl's state of mind; she didn't expect to escape this despite what the nice man had said. She hadn't learned yet to really trust the manifestations. Resignation enveloped her face.

"You can do this!"And Rachel hoped she could too.

The water was beginning to make her feet feel lighter as it tried to lift her from the bridge. Her left hand had a death grip on the railing while her right reached out to a child about to give up.

"Now!" The girl reached up out of the water as far as she could, first grasping at thin air and then latching onto Rachel's hand.

"I've got you," Rachel said. "Hold on!" She lifted her up. Soaked in water, she was heavier than Rachel expected. Her hand tightened. There was no letting go now.

The little one was still dangerously close to washing under the bridge. Her legs had already disappeared beneath it. She was tired and her grip didn't feel secure. Rachel took the risk of using both hands to pull her up. With a herculean effort, she pulled the girl from the river and deposited her on the bridge.

"Can you run? Is anything broken?"

The swollen river covered their shoes.

Her head nodded rapidly.

Still clutching hands, Rachel ran practically dragging the exhausted girl. When she reached the other side of Alameda, she stopped.

"Can you ride piggy-back?"

The girl nodded.

"Get on. We have to run."

Rachel looked back once as the river flowed onto the street and across it. She ran with all the strength of surging adrenalin and didn't stop until they reached the Plaza.

People were congregating in the downtown park, all looking back in the direction of the river, hoping it didn't come any farther into the city.

Rachel carefully put the child down.

"Kid, what's your name?" she asked while cautiously patting her arms and legs for any broken bones. She didn't know if that was effective, but felt she had to do something.

"Anna. My name is Anna." Her teeth were chattering. Cold or fear?

"Well Anna, you did great. I'm proud of you. Thank you for trusting me."

She nodded.

"Does anything hurt?" Rachel tried again.

Anna pointed to her head where there was a small lump forming. Out of the water, it was beginning to bleed.

"Is that all?"

Another nod.

"Okay sweetie." Rachel didn't know how to talk to kids, but one of her friends was a second grade teacher and she'd heard her talk to her students this way. It was worth a try.

"I'm going to get you to a doctor. Do you know where your parents are?"

She pointed east, but that didn't tell Rachel much.

"We'll find them. Don't worry. Now jump up again.

There is a doctor nearby." Anna obediently complied.

Rachel race-walked down Palace to a nearby minor ER. It was a long 10 minutes, but she cut through a parking lot to shorten the trek. Traffic was stopped on Paseo de Peralta due to the flooding. She took advantage and crossed quickly. Her shoes were already ruined. A little more water didn't matter.

Placing Anna on the sidewalk, they burst into the clinic.

"I need help!" Rachel shouted. "This child nearly drowned in the river."

The receptionist called out to a nurse who came running.

"Come on," Rachel grabbed Anna's hand.

"Don't leave me," she pleaded.

"No chance. You're stuck with me."

Tenderly, Rachel lifted Anna onto the exam table. A doctor rushed in and she stepped back to the wall that gratefully held her up. She was about to crumple. Adrenalin spent, she felt like a wet noodle, sagging in the middle.

Anna looked at her, eyes wide.

"You're okay. Just let them help you." Rachel quickly explained what happened, and then called 9-1-1 to get assistance finding Anna's parents.

"How old are you?" the doctor asked.

Anna held up four fingers.

"What's your name?"

"Anna."

"What's your last name?" the doctor asked hopefully.

Anna glanced at Rachel.

"I don't think she knows," Rachel said. "Is that right?"

Anna nodded again.

"It's okay. We're going to find them."

The 9-1-1 operator answered. Rachel hurriedly explained. They were busy. She could hear the chaos in the background as the operators quickly tried to get help on the way to the many emergency calls.

"She looks okay, but I want to keep her here for awhile because of the bump on the head," the doctor said. "We've got a room where she can lie down. I've checked her eyes; no dilation. She can answer questions. Those are good signs."

"Can I stay with her?"

"Absolutely." He smiled reassuringly at Anna who bravely tried to smile back.

When settled, Anna went to sleep.

Without taking her eyes off Anna, Rachel used the phone in the room to call Jules and dictated the story as he recorded it.

"Headline," she said. "Swept Away: Santa Fe River Floods." She added several paragraphs including the fish kill, the yellow color of the water and the rescue of Anna, but left her name out of it."

"Am I to conclude, you want to be left out of it?" Jules asked.

"I think so."

"How about I say a High Desert Country reporter was involved in the rescue?"

"Okay," she acquiesced.

"Rachel," Jules tone was soft. "You did good. Are you staying with the girl?"

"Yeah. Until her parents arrive. The police are looking for them now."

"Come in late tomorrow. You earned it."

"Jules, one thing."

"Yes?"

"If you hadn't asked me to do this story, I hate to think ... people were running away," Rachel choked a little.

"Don't think about it. I did and you did. We have a happy ending."

Rachel hung up and began to cry. Nothing loud and ugly, but tears streamed down her cheeks as she wiped them angrily away with her hands. Taking a deep breath seemed to help calm the shock she was feeling. She crawled onto the table with Anna and wrapped her arms around the girl in the smelly, damp clothing.

Anna stirred.

"What is your name?" she asked.

"I'm Rachel."

"You're Rachel?"

"Yes. Why?"

"The man told me. Let the woman, Rachel, rescue you."

"What man?"

"He was over the water. He told me not to be afraid, but I was."

"That's okay Anna; it was an afraid kind of thing."

"What did the man look like?" Rachel asked

"He was old with long white hair." Anna struggled to explain not knowing all the words.

"He said to tell you ...

"Tell me what?"

"It's the cats-ee-nah," she sounded it out.

"Did he say anything else?" Rachel prompted.

"Let the powder go through you." Anna was tiring and fell back to sleep without realizing she had misstated the message.

Rachel wiped at her eyes. She was fairly sure that the shaman Joseph had made a spiritual appearance. She hadn't seen anyone but Anna in the river. But if it was him, what did the cryptic messages mean? Maybe she could sort it out later. She closed her eyes.

A few minutes later, the nurse came in, took Anna's pulse and felt her forehead. Satisfied, she picked up a blanket and covered the two sleeping people.

Chapter 17

Anna's parents showed up an hour later. The police found them standing on a picnic table down the river. They rescued them with a boat. After checking with dispatch they learned where their daughter was and took the couple to the clinic.

The nurse showed them into the quiet room. Rachel woke and smiled at the man and woman who were obviously terribly upset and very relieved. She squeezed Anna's hand.

"Your parents are here. You're okay now," Rachel told her. "You were brave today; a real warrior princess."

Anna beamed.

Her parents cried and hugged the little girl over and over.

"'Bye sweetie." Rachel tried to slip out the door, but Anna ran to her and hugged her legs. Rachel squatted to be on her level.

"It's the cats-ee-nah," Anna repeated. "You'll remember?"

"Yes Anna. I will remember. And Anna, if you see the man again, ask if his name is Joseph."

"Okay."

"What man?" Anna's mother said alarmed. "There was a man?"

"He was helping her," Rachel explained. "No one to be afraid of." She didn't want Anna to have to explain. It was clear that someone, possibly Joseph, had appeared to her. If the child was clairvoyant, she didn't want her parents worrying about her anymore than they already had.

"Here Anna, take this." Rachel tugged a business card out of her pocket. "Call me, anytime you want."

Anna's mother relaxed and she hugged her daughter again.

"Thank you," she said to Rachel. "Thank you."

"My pleasure. You have a brave girl." She winked at Anna.

When Rachel exited the clinic, it was as if nothing had happened. Cars were driving past. Sediment, twigs and grass had washed and were now left in small piles, but no fish had reached this far. People were walking about again, but she caught scraps of excited conversation. Some had narrow escapes with the water; others wanted to know what was going on.

As for Rachel, she wanted a shower and a cold beer. But first, she had to cross the river again. Alameda had been flooded. The pavement was wet, mud made curly patterns where it had settled as the water receded. She carefully crossed the road and stepped up on the curb to get a look at the river. It was only half-full now, but the grass that grew within its banks had been flattened by the powerful water. Dead fish were everywhere along the riverbanks and in the canal. Drivers were trying to go around them on Alameda. In a couple of hours, it would smell really bad.

Rachel opened her canvas purse, pulled out a plastic sandwich bag with her few cosmetics inside. She dumped them in the dark interior. Carefully inching her way down to the water surface, she scooped up some of the yellow water and zipped the plastic sack.

She crossed the bridge where she pulled Anna to safety. The urge to cry surfaced again. But movement caught her attention. A fish lying on the bridge was moving. Carefully, she picked it up and let it go in the receding river.

"Good luck," Rachel whispered. She threw her shoulders back and hurried to the other side. Once in the Merc, she headed home.

Chile Pod greeted her as she came through the garage door to the kitchen. A look of concern flashed over her face. Her nose twitched, trying to identify this new odor. Rachel realized how she must look. She'd gotten wet even though she hadn't been in the flood. She dropped the river water sample into the sink.

"I'm going to take a shower."

Chile Pod followed her to the bathroom. She sat quietly on the rug and waited while Rachel washed the experience from her body.

It felt good to get clean. But while no one was around to see her, she thanked the Universe for its help. Rachel wasn't religious, but she threw a thank you out there with frequency. She had no clue if anyone was listening, but it felt good to be grateful. And then without warning, she sobbed, letting the water wash away her tears. It was with much relief that little Anna would have a chance to grow up. She had been able to stand her ground and help the girl. She felt there would always be a bond between them.

The phone rang while she toweled off. Wrapping it around her, she hurried to answer.

"Hello."

"Rachel, do you know what just happened?" Chloe asked excitedly.

"In fact, I do."

Rachel told her the quick version.

"Are you okay?" The concern in her friend's voice made Rachel feel cared for.

"Yes, I'm okay. Just had a shower and about to dry my hair."

"You need food," Chloe said. "I'll be right over. Do you have beer?"

Rachel opened the fridge revealed one lonely Negra Modelo.

"I'll pick up some," Chloe said. "Don't do anything strenuous. You're probably a little shocky. See you soon. Kiss. Kiss." Chloe was gone.

"That was Auntie Chloe," she told Chile Pod who had followed her into the kitchen. "She's bringing food."

When Chloe arrived she carried the scent of Santa Fe: salads with candied pecans and blue cheese, pollo adovada, cheese enchiladas, pinto beans and flan for dessert. And there was an assorted six-pack, cold and ready to drink. They made their choices and sat down at the kitchen table. Chile Pod had her meal of adovada and cheese garnish on the kitchen counter.

"I'm sorry for what you went through," Chloe said. "But I'm elated that you and the little girl are okay."

"Thanks," Rachel said embarrassed. "I didn't have much choice. Everyone else was trying to get away and if they saw Anna, they just kept on running."

"Regardless, you did it!" Chloe said. "Anna's parents still have their child; thanks to you."

Despite not being a parent, nor wanting to be, Rachel had to admit she was very glad the rescue had been successful. Her feelings were mixed, but they felt good.

"What do you make of Anna's messages?" Chloe asked.

"Let the powder go through you?" Rachel repeated. "I immediately thought of that fibre supplement, you know, for regularity?"

They both laughed; and it felt good to let go for a few minutes.

"Well, we know it has to mean more than that," Chloe finally got herself together.

"She also said, 'It's the cats-ee-nah.' "That sounds so familiar," Rachel mused. "I'll have to let that settle in until it makes sense."

"Say, why do you think Joseph contacted Anna? If it was Joseph," Rachel asked.

"I was reading something the other day about Indigo and Crystal children," Chloe said. "Most of the Indigo children began arriving in the 1970s. In the 1990s they were followed by the Crystal children. The Crystals are endowed with psychic gifts and sometimes they prefer to communicate in ways other than speech. It may be through telepathy, rocking or singing. They may be labeled as autistic or as having Asperger's syndrome.

"You mentioned that she didn't talk much," Chloe continued. "That can be a sign of a Crystal child. And it's one of the reasons they may be diagnosed incorrectly.

They are old souls and what's going on in their spiritual realm is far more important than talking."

"That would explain how a spirit was able to reach her," Rachel said. "And pass on information through her. If only I understood the message."

CHAPTER 18

They ate in silence. It tasted like the best meal Rachel had ever eaten. Everything always tasted better, the sun looked brighter and the birds sang sweeter after a close call. She could feel the adrenalin losing its punch as she came down and began to tire.

"Where did the yellow water come from?" Chloe asked.

"No clue, but I'm going to find out. I got a sample on the way home."

"Rachel, that's great. What made you think of that?"

"Something's very wrong," Rachel said. "First the bird kills, the otherworldly appearance in my backyard, his prediction, the deaths of the university grad students, and now being in the right place at the right time to rescue Anna. And there is the ever closer Dog Star.

"My understanding is the yellow water and fish kill is another sign of the impending end of the Fourth World."

They were thoughtful for a few minutes.

"Rachel, I wonder," Chloe said. "Should we visit the Valles Caldera? Is there anything we could learn there?"

"I think there might be," Rachel said thoughtfully. "The last time I was there I did an interview for the *Longmire* TV series coverage, back when they were filming in New Mexico. We ran several stories on that production. The Valles Caldera was used as Sheriff Longmire's ranch location."

"Quite a drive from the Las Vegas where they filmed the downtown and sheriff's office scenes," Chloe said.

"Yes, I know. I drove to both sets for the interviews

and again to Madrid and the Mine Shaft Tavern that was used as the Red Pony bar."

"I hated when that series ended," Chloe said.

"Yup, me too. Seems like the good shows always end too soon."

"And *Supernatural*," Chloe added. "Don't know what we'll do without Sam and Dean to guide us on these, uh, mystical excursions."

"At least they got 15 years," Rachel said.

Rachel changed the subject.

"You know, I've had those herb plants sitting on my back porch all summer. I think after what happened today, I'd like to do a little gardening."

"You want help?" Chloe asked.

Rachel raised an eyebrow in question. She'd never seen Chloe plant any of her gardens.

"Well, I could ask my gardener if he would have time to plant it for you."

Rachel grinned.

"No; but thank you for the offer. I think I need to do something physical."

"Okay," Chloe said. "I'm going to check in at the office, see if anything critical is afoot and then go home to a hot bath and a glass of wine."

"Do you think they will still grow?" Rachel asked.

"What?"

"The herbs."

"Sure, everything but the parsley will likely come back in the spring. Sometimes my parsley overwinters," Chloe said. "Of course, as you so kindly pointed out I don't cultivate my own so my gardener may have secrets to plant longevity I don't know."

"I just can't see anything else dead for awhile," Rachel choked.

"I know," Chloe said and hugged her friend. "Seeing those poor men will haunt us both for a long time. Go get your hands dirty and forget about today.

"I'll let myself out." Chloe was gone in a whirl of her long dark hair.

Chile Pod had finished her dinner and was keeping watch via the kitchen window. A bird picked at seeds that had fallen to the ground.

"You stay there. You can watch me plant the herb bed." Rachel grabbed a jacket off the hook near the door and went into the evening air.

She'd bought the herb plants in spring and somehow never got around to planting them, but remembered to douse them with water several times a week. There never was a good time to plant them. Now the leggy plants were root bound. Rachel hoped she could save them.

Months ago, in a fit of energy, she had turned the soil and laid bricks in a 6-foot square bed. In the meantime, deadlines came and went. Time passed without planting the herbs.

Because she had mulched the garden to prevent weeds, all she had to do was push the organic matter away, dig a hole and add the plants. First, Rachel took a knife and cut the roots back as she remembered her father doing when she was a kid. It would help the roots grow in a more normal way. She planted lavender and then added rosemary, thyme, oregano and fennel.

With that done, Rachel picked up the bucket against her house and brought it to the garden. Inside were an assortment of stones and crystals she had collected for the past several years. She placed each amongst the herbs; a river stone here, a quartz crystal there and a lovely piece of petrified wood.

When it was all watered in, Rachel went inside the house and came back with several gazing balls in purple, blue and red crackled colors. In the center of the herb bed she placed a stand and added the larger purple gazing ball. She positioned the smaller ones on the ground and stood back to survey her handiwork.

Satisfied and feeling better, she headed back inside. Before she reached the safety of the backdoor, a wolf howled. Rachel was now recognizing the various warnings that Kiyiya made to alert her. This howl was an announcement, not an urgent warning.

Rachel stopped, her pulse quickened and her breath turned to fog as the temperature dropped. Once again, the rattling sound commenced, the vapors seemingly came from nowhere and formed into a column. She had no idea who or what to expect. Would it be the Native American she met most recently or someone or something altogether different?

It was the Native who stepped from the fog. Rachel braced herself and waited.

“The blue star grows in the sky,” he pointed.

“I know,” Rachel replied. “What I don’t know is who or what is causing it?”

“The evil men.”

“Who are the evil men? What are they doing to cause the star to come closer?” Rachel asked.

“I do not know them,” he said. “They are of this time. Not of mine.”

“Do you know what they are doing that is wrong?”

“Taking from our land.”

This wasn’t going well. There was a lot of time and space between them. Rachel didn’t know if she could span the centuries. She tried to keep her words simple to enhance his comprehension.

“I’ve been looking for these men, but haven’t found them. I’ve looked to see where ... where work is being done. I’ve checked for mining and drilling permits.”

“I don’t understand,” he said.

“I’m sorry. It’s when men remove treasures by digging into the ground.” He nodded.

“I’ve been trying to uncover what these men are doing along with two friends who are helping me. And I think that two men were killed who may have known what I need to know.”

The man was silent for several minutes. Rachel thought he was about to disappear leaving her in more confusion.

“Do your powers take you to the Land of the Dead?” he asked.

That took her off guard.

“I ... I,” she stammered. “I don’t know.”

“You must talk with the Skeleton Man.”

"Can I do that? I don't know how." Rachel asked.

"You have friends in spirit?" he said as though having inside knowledge.

"Uh, yes." As far as Rachel knew that would be one spirit. The Hopi shaman, Joseph,

"You should talk with spirit," the Native said. "Time grows ... " He searched for the word. "Short. Everyone will die."

"I understand, but I don't know what to do," Rachel felt panic seeping into her soul.

"You must talk with Skeleton Man." He faded from her view in a whiff of smoke.

"Dammit!" she said. "All I get are riddles and mumbo-jumbo. How am I supposed to solve this mystery and save the world? And why the hell does it have to be me?"

Inside, Rachel turned on cable news to find the anchor talking about the Dog Star.

... scientists say they don't know why the Dog Star is moving ever closer to the Earth. But we are getting reports of star gazers gathering outside cities to watch it. In Sedona, Arizona, some are performing rituals they hope will return it to its normal track. We know that NASA has been keeping close watch and the US military is on alert. For now, the mystery deepens as to the reason and potential outcome.

The accompanying video of the star showed where it normally was and how close it was currently.

An interview with Dr. Saxon in the *Albuquerque Journal* had been picked up by the wire services. He was interviewed for the segment.

Here in New Mexico we are concerned not just with Sirius, but also the recurrence of earthquakes in the area near the Los Alamos National Laboratory. It's very near the LANL but we don't know if the movement of Sirius is linked. While there have been connections made with the moon and earthquakes, we don't know if a star could cause this. We're still gathering data and evaluating it.

Footage of the LANL and the Valles Caldera were shown during his interview.

Rachel opted for an early bedtime. Chile Pod crawled under the covers and snuggled against her; Rachel absently rubbed her head and was rewarded with a robust purr. But Rachel couldn't stop her incessant thoughts as she tried to comprehend what was happening and how she fit into the upshot.

Before today, she hadn't connected the earthquakes to the Dog Star's new astral behavior. What if it was connected? If one was stopped would the other be halted too? The only thing she knew for sure; time was an essential dynamic and it was running short.

CHAPTER 19

Being a journalist has its perks; certainly not the salary, but in resources and information. Not only were websites open to her that the general public couldn't access, she had a wealth of contacts from interviews she had done over the years. Having written many stories on New Mexico's water issues, Rachel had run across a testing facility. It has been the focus of a story she did a couple of years ago when covering water quality in the City Different. She dropped her river sample off on the way to work, running up her credit card the equivalent of a couple of Benjamin Franklins.

When she crossed the threshold to the *High Desert Country* publication office, Stella greeted her.

"Hi hon. Heard about your adventure yesterday. Are you okay?"

"Uh yes," Rachel replied. "No harm."

"Brave thing you did," Stella whispered. "I'm proud of you."

Rachel couldn't remember the last time she had heard those words. Maybe before her dad died. It wasn't often. It caught her off guard and she felt her eyes swimming.

"Oh sweetie." Stella came around the desk and wrapped Rachel in her arms. "Didn't mean to make you cry."

"I'm not crying," Rachel protested, but she was.

"That took courage when everyone else was running away," Stella said. "You did good, girl." She shook Rachel slightly for emphasis.

"Thank you." Rachel didn't know what else to say. "The

important thing is that little Anna lived to play another day," she managed between sobs.

"And our friend and co-worker lived to write another day." Stella added. "Okay, off you go, before we get all girly nauseous." Stella always seemed to know what to say and when to stop saying it.

Rachel ran up the stairs to her office, but before she could get to work, Jules stopped by.

"Saw that encounter with Stella," he said rubbing his beard. "Wish you'd let me name you in the story, but I know you don't want that." He raised his hands in acquiescence. "But you did good kid. Now, get to work."

"Thanks Jules."

Rachel sat at her desk a few minutes head in hands as she waited to change hats from reluctant hero to writer. She pulled up the story on Bandelier and began writing a sidebar about the deaths of the men from the University of New Mexico, the earthquake activity, the menacing Valles Caldera and the massive damage that could occur. Since she couldn't connect the Dog Star scientifically with the ongoing events around Bandelier she didn't include it, but hoped for a confirmation later.

Jules might not publish it as it wasn't a likely piece for his magazine. But she wanted it down while it was fresh and organized in her mind. Just writing a rough draft and saving it was important. Most of what a reporter does is not writing, but interviewing, research and collecting small amounts of information that may fill in the dots later for a full picture.

She would write it as a sidebar. But if it wasn't a fit for *High Desert*, it might make a better stand-alone piece for a larger news publication. Jules was okay with that. As events unfolded, she would add the results of the water test and any illegal mining or drilling she might uncover that related to the seismic activity. She was convinced something illegal was at the root of these issues.

Stella buzzed her out of her thoughts.

"Rachel, line three. It's that sweet Chloe."

"Thanks Stella."

"Hello sweet Chloe," Rachel said.

"It's Stella who's sweet," Chloe cooed.

Fearing getting stuck in another complimentary loop between these two Rachel interrupted.

"What's up?"

"The weekend is practically upon us. Let's plan our trip to the Valles Caldera. How about we leave Saturday morning about ten?"

"I think that's a good idea," Rachel said. "Maybe there is something there that will shed light on this."

"We have to try," Chloe said. "Doing nothing will only result in the end of the world."

"We must understand," Rachel added. "Even if we do everything we can, we still may fail."

"Not in my vocabulary," Chloe retorted. "See you at ten."

Rachel hung up the phone. She wasn't as confident as Chloe. Failure was occasionally found in her vocabulary.

* * *

Saturday dawned clear, bright and beautiful.

They soon covered the less than 20 miles on Highway 4 west of Los Alamos and parked along the road. A trio of signs announced that they had arrived at their destination. It would be necessary to walk the rest of the way to the Valles Caldera cabin as the preserve currently did not allow vehicle traffic.

"It's about a two-mile hike to the *Longmire* cabin," Rachel said.

"I happen to have on my new hiking boots," Chloe stuck out her foot.

"The boots you bought from the cute guy at REI?"

"The very ones."

Rachel handed Chloe a reflective vest from her backpack and grabbed another for herself. She used them when covering stories along highways and construction areas.

"It's hunting season. We don't want to be a target," Rachel said.

"Oh great," Chloe exclaimed. "Why does everything have to be complicated?"

"Hard to avoid hunting season this time of year," Rachel said. "It basically runs from September through the end of the year. Mostly elk and there are plenty of them around here."

Rachel grabbed her pepper spray from her bag just in case they ran into any scary creatures. They began to walk the gravel road that led to the cabin. It was mostly level, but did have a slight incline. It would be easier coming back.

The cabins appeared along with a sign unnecessarily announcing "Entering Cabin District." They crossed a cattle guard and it wasn't long before the iconic cabin came into view.

"That was faster than I thought," Chloe said, breathing somewhat heavily.

"It would have been quicker had you not jumped at every sound along the way."

"I read about a bear attack and was just being careful."

"That's why I have this," Rachel pulled out the pepper spray.

"You could have told me," Chloe pouted.

The porch of the *Longmire* cabin with the magnificent view of the caldera was open today. Maybe the rangers forgot to hang the sign prohibiting entry. Rachel and Chloe walked up the steps and looked inside the front window at the familiar room they'd seen in the series. Where Robert Taylor had played the out of tune piano and downed a few Rainier beers.

"Guess that's it," Chloe said as she tried the locked door.

"We can sit on the steps and appreciate the sight," Rachel said making herself comfortable on the top step.

"It is gorgeous," Chloe observed.

"Yes," Rachel agreed. "We can't see all the caldera because Redondo Peak, the resurgent dome, obscures the far side. Supervolcanoes are actually called super eruptions by scientists because they are formed by multiple volcanoes that interact. The Toledo caldera intersects the Valles. Smaller lava domes form a half-circle on the north side."

Rachel sat quietly for a few minutes watching a herd of

elk entering the caldera and beginning to graze. The caldera didn't look frightening at all, but more like peaceful pasture land encircled by mountains. If you didn't know what to look for, you'd never know it was anything other than a bucolic valley.

Something was up with the elk. Many had alerted; their heads raised and ears forward. She hoped they would not witness hunters killing any of them.

"Rachel," Chloe said. "Is that fog that's forming around the peak?"

Before she could answer, there was a rumbling sound. A few seconds later the ground was shaking. The elk herd made a dash for the forest. They disappeared into the trees. Rachel hoped they would be safe.

"Let's get away from the house," Chloe shouted.

They squatted on the ground to keep from falling.

"I thought I was going to be sick," Chloe shouted. "Didn't realize it was an earthquake.

The ground beneath them swayed and a crack opened. As the shaking continued the crack would almost close and then reopen.

Rachel looked up at Redondo.

"That's not fog. That's smoke! Run for the car!"

They did the best they could while the ground continued to wobble. Rachel tried to distract herself by counting. When she reached 47 seconds, the ground stopped moving. They paused and looked at the mountain blowing off steam. When it was over, they had barely escaped the cabin area because it was so difficult to run.

"Is it going to blow?" Chloe asked.

"Can't answer that," Rachel replied. "Make tracks."

Twenty-five minutes later they reached the car breathing hard. The shaking had slowly come to a stop, but the ground quivered repeatedly.

"That's the best time I've ever made on two miles," Chloe said looking up at Redondo Peak. "It seems to have stopped smoking."

"Healthier for all of us," Rachel tried for humor, but she couldn't laugh.

That's when they noticed the SUV parked on the other side of the road. A man was shoving some items under a tarp. He likely wanted to get away too. But Rachel stopped short of getting in the vehicle.

"Hi," she said. "Dr. Saxon?"

He looked up, closed the back and walked quickly to Rachel and Chloe.

"Hi Rachel. What on earth are you two doing out here?" he sounded irritated. "Even I was about to leave, but I'm waiting on my crew."

"What crew?" Rachel looked about.

"Oh, they're in the trees over there checking instruments and then we're heading out."

"This is my friend Chloe," Rachel said. "Dr. Saxon from the University of New Mexico's geology department."

They shook hands quickly.

"You two should leave," Saxon said. "We don't know if it's over for now or might start shaking again.

"He's right, Rachel," Chloe said. "Let's go."

"Take care," Rachel said to Saxon.

"How close do you think we came?" Chloe asked once in the car.

"Maybe Saxon will let me know. For now, we could still be in danger."

* * *

When they reached Santa Fe they parked a few blocks away from The Shed. It was late in the afternoon and the restaurant was opening for the dinner crowd. Rachel and Chloe found two seats at the bar and ordered.

Chloe's phone rang.

"It's for you," she handed the cell to Rachel.

"Yes. Rachel here."

"Rachel, this is Stella. I just picked up a message for you from the office voice mail." Stella's voice sounded anxious. And if she and Chloe didn't do their sickening back and forth complimentary blitz, there must be something wrong.

"What is it Stella?" Rachel prompted.

"Dr. Saxon from UMN left you a message saying the university's seismograph 'went nuts' this afternoon. A 5.6 in earthquake speak. He said it was located in the Espanola Basin along the Rio Grande Rift. Do you know what he's talking about?"

"Afraid I do," Rachel said.

"And one other thing," Stella continued. "He said the worst of it was between Bandelier and Redondo Peak in the Valles Caldera. Do we need to worry?"

"I don't know, but I wouldn't tell you to put it out of your mind."

"Is this something you're working on for the paper?" Stella asked.

"Yes and no, but mostly yes," Rachel tried to give a non-explanation explanation. "And thank you Stella for checking in on the weekend and tracking me down. It's important."

"So I thought. You two be careful; and I mean that," Stella said.

"We will. Thank you. See you Monday."

Rachel handed the phone back to Chloe.

"You have got to get a cell phone Rachel."

"Why? You're always around with yours." Rachel related the message.

"Wow, a 5.6," Chloe echoed. "It was quite a rumble.

"But I don't understand," Chloe continued. "Why did he call when he saw us awhile ago at the caldera?"

"Guess his crew came back with the information and he wanted the magazine to know what the strength was," Rachel said. "It is pertinent to the story."

"Something disturbing happened after you left the other night," Rachel said changing the subject.

"What now? Everything the past few weeks has been disturbing." Chloe said with concern.

"The Ancient Puebloan paid me a visit after I finished the herb bed."

"What did he say?" Chloe asked leaning in.

"He said I had to talk with the Skeleton Man."

"The Hopi Lord of the Dead? Másaw? Oh my god!"

"I know," Rachel agreed. "Thing is, I don't know how to find him, let alone talk with him."

Chloe was thoughtful for a moment, sipping her cranberry margarita that she insisted was healthier than the regular house version.

"I think I know how you can get to him."

"And ... ?" Rachel waited.

"You'll need to do a vision quest. That's the only way I think it's possible."

"A vision quest?" Rachel was incredulous. "I don't even know if non-Natives are allowed to do that."

"Rachel, the whole fucking world is going to end if we don't figure this out. And from the size of the Dog Star, I don't think we have much time."

"I know," Rachel said with resignation. "I'll call Dominic and see what he knows about them."

"Don't put it off Rachel. I'm getting scared."

"You and me both."

CHAPTER 20

The next morning Rachel was up early and called Dominic. He answered on the fourth ring and sounded sleepy.

"Sorry, did I wake you?" Rachel asked.

"What time is it?" She could see him smoothing his rumbled hair.

"Again, I'm so sorry, but it is important," Rachel said.

"Come on over. I'll make us some breakfast."

By the time Rachel pulled the Merc into Dominic's drive, he had made scrambled eggs, hash browns, whole grain toast and a pan of green chile heating.

Juan, his Chihuahua, unleashed everything he had, taking his role of guard dog way over the top. When Rachel reached out to him, he took one sniff and excitedly welcomed her. It was almost as loud as his first rollout.

Dominic poured tea and they sat down to a small Santa Fe *desayuno* feast. Rachel found that she was hungry and wolfed down the plate of food she had drowned in chile.

"That was delicious." She sipped her tea.

Dominic was only about half-finished with his breakfast. Rachel was a bit embarrassed that she had eaten so quickly.

"Tell me," Dominic began. "Does the important thing include the Dog Star and its ever looming presence?"

"Yes."

"I checked my newsfeed before you arrived and NPR says that Sirius is beginning to spiral in its descent to Earth."

"What does that indicate?"

"In Native American culture the spiral symbolizes the

evolution of our planet. You could say it appears when a cleansing is needed," Dominic explained.

"That really resonates with what is going on." Rachel sighed.

"Dominic, I was told by a spirit that I needed to talk with the Skeleton Man in the Land of the Dead."

Dominic whistled slow and low.

"Look, I know you've, well visited, with spirits before, but going to the Land of the Dead is a whole different level of spirit world. It could be dangerous. This isn't a cross-cultural exchange program you're talking about."

"I know," Rachel said exasperated. "I don't know why this has landed in my lap, but it has and obviously I have to follow through to the end."

"Because if you don't the world will end for all of us?" Dominic asked.

"Yes. The Ancient Puebloan told me that we would all die if I didn't stop bad men from doing something, but he gave me very little information about how I find and stop them.

Rachel told Dominic about the night she and Chloe camped out. She nodded at his questioning expression. After raising his eyebrows in surprise at the mental picture of Chloe camping, he listened intently. She related the incident with the intimidating men and their discovery of clandestine goings on in the Bandelier wilderness.

"Do you think the murder of the two UNM grad students is related?"

"That would be my guess," Rachel said.

"Look, Chloe thinks the only way for me to enter the Land of the Dead is through a vision quest. What do you think? Could a mostly Caucasian woman do this?

"I honestly can't say if it's ever happened," Dominic said. "But I'm with Chloe on this. I don't see another way. You need to contact your crystal medicine woman and get, not only protection for you, but protection for the dead."

"You mean I have to protect them from me, right?"

"Yes."

Dominic pushed back his chair and searched his bookshelves.

“Here, this should educate you on the basic steps to a vision quest. This second text should give you an idea of what to expect in the Land of the Dead, keeping in mind that these are stories handed down verbally through the generations. No one that I know of has ever attempted to do what you are considering.

Rachel took the books and walked to the front door.

“Thank you for breakfast and these.” She looked at the books in her hand.

“Rachel.” Dominic rested both hands on her shoulders. “This isn’t a séance in your basement with friends; this is an excursion into the spirit realm. Probably unlike any you have experienced yet. You will likely be unwelcome. Spirits and other entities may try to trick you and even hurt you. You have to know you might not come back from this.”

CHAPTER 21

Home alone in her office corner tucked into the breakfast nook of her kitchen, Rachel read the chapters on how to perform a vision quest.

She picked up the phone and called Chloe.

"Hello Rach. What's up?"

"Chloe, we have to talk. I think we need Mari-Lynn. Dominic gave me information on performing a vision quest and entering the Land of the Dead. I've got to have protection and I must protect the inhabitants from me as well."

"It happens our favorite medicine woman and pot dealer is moving to Santa Fe," Chloe replied. "In fact, I think her pot business is open and she stocking the crystal store."

"What? Really!"

"Yes, she's opened a medical cannabis dispensary here in the Railroad District," Chloe explained. "Her partner Celeste is running it. No problem getting supply. She has fields of primo shit in Colorado."

"Hey, she's going legit?" Rachel asked. "Say, is it legal to import grass from out of state?"

"Don't know," Chloe said. "But Mari-Lynn has been successfully outwitting the law for a couple of decades. She will make it work."

"This year medicinal is legal," Rachel added. "Perhaps next year; recreational?"

"Not only that, but the Mari-Lynn is opening a store next door called Chrysalis where she will sell crystals, sage bundles and a variety of other spiritual items," Chloe said. "Both stores are on side streets just off Guadalupe. Shall I give her a call and see if she can help us?"

"Please do. We don't have much time. Dominic said the Dog Star is beginning to spiral and that could mean a collision with Earth is nearing."

"Are you kidding me?" Chloe asked. "I haven't seen any news today."

"Sadly no."

"Okay," Chloe said. "I've got her new number. I'll give her a call and see if she can help us."

Twenty minutes later the two were on their way to the Railyard in Chloe's new car, a red Lexus sport model.

"Geez," Rachel said. "This looks like a cockpit. Does it fly?"

"Almost," Chloe smiled. "Listen to that purr when I accelerate." Rachel looked at her friend with the satisfied grin on her face.

"But, this is too small to haul clients," Rachel questioned. "There's almost no backseat."

"Still have the big Mercedes for clients or I could always borrow your mammoth Marquis," Chloe said. "You know, Mercury isn't made anymore. Who knows how long you will be able to get parts."

Rachel frowned at her friend from the comfy seat with its own temperature control, seat warmer and curtain of air bags. She wouldn't give Chloe the satisfaction, but she thought she could get used to this.

Chloe was talking again. "This car is all mine. It has satellite radio, state-of-the-art entertainment system and navigation. Get's terrible gas mileage and I don't give a rat's ass!"

She pushed a button and a disembodied woman's voice inquired as to what she wanted.

"Classic Vinyl," Chloe replied. The radio played Led Zeppelin's "Kashmir."

"This is broadcast from the Rock 'n Roll Hall of Fame in Cleveland," She said smugly.

"Here we go," Rachel said drolly. "Chloe has a new toy."

It felt conspiratorial to laugh and they did as they rocked their way to Mari-Lynn's new establishment.

"And if real estate bottoms out, which doesn't look plausible for now, I can always sell the car to eat," Chloe giggled some more. She made a turn.

"I think it's down this street," Chloe maneuvered the smart little car into a parallel parking place and they got out.

"Wow," Chloe said. "Mari-Lynn's going all out, but with all that money she raked in when pot was illegal, she probably has greenbacks stacked floor to the ceiling in a Colorado cave."

A tasteful shingle hung on a stained wood post near the street with a monarch butterfly carefully painted next to the name.

Chrysalis was in an adobe house with a wood coyote fence surrounding it, but missing a gate. Invitingly landscaped in desert flora, the pathway was large flat stones surrounded by brown pea gravel. Purple asters bloomed along the path intermixed with ornamental grasses, sagebrush and blooming chamisa. Rachel held her breath passing by the chamisa. She was allergic to the yellow blooms, which she thought smelled terrible. But it was a beautiful shrub in autumn mingled among the piñon and sagebrush that dotted the northern New Mexico landscape.

After they walked the short path to the front door they were welcomed by a much larger butterfly on the door. This was a work of art, created in mosaic tile of orange, black and white embedded in a lapis background. There was a long portal with a swing and chairs to relax in. The courtyard carried on the desert landscaping but a fish pond was the main attraction. Water flowed over more stones and made the most calming sound as it ran off the rock ledge and tumbled into the pool. Koi in bright hues of orange, red, white and black splotches swam peacefully in their new home. This would be a popular reading spot and there was enough space for an outdoor sale.

A discreet sign informed them the store was closed. They knocked.

Within seconds, Mari-Lynn emerged from behind a display and made her way to the door in flowing gauzy garments and silver waist-length hair.

In Santa Fe, women rock their grey hair. No one thinks less of a woman who doesn't color her hair. In fact, it goes great with turquoise jewelry and hats of all kinds, a necessity in the high desert city.

Today Mari-Lynn wore a turquoise squash blossom necklace and a silver cuff. Her dress was constructed in layers of light cotton with an over shirt. In pastel colors of mauve and blue the fabric stirred like clouds on currents of air as she moved.

"Welcome Chloe and Rachel, my first customers." She closed the door and locked it behind them.

"This is beautiful!" Chloe said admiring the store's interior.

"And Rachel," Mari-Lynn said. "I will be serving both coffee and tea."

"Thanks for thinking of us tea drinkers," Rachel responded.

She pointed to the corner of the store where the open space made an "L" next to her office. Lining the many shelves were books and more books. In the center there were comfy chairs and a sofa draped in amazing throws of southwest colors: azure, yellow and glorious reds. Reading lamps completed the cozy spot. Mari-Lynn had thought of everything.

"I'm going to the animal shelter later and adopt two cats for the shop," Mari-Lynn said. "I've already picked them out from their website: Mesquite and Cholla. Their beds, food and water bowls and private litter boxes await them. Even have food and treats. The whole property is fenced and I'm going to add a gate to the front in a couple of days so they can go outside and sun in the courtyard. They're getting their ID chips today.

"Mari-Lynn," Rachel said. "This is fabulous. I'm so happy for you."

"Only one more thing to work out," Mari-Lynn said. "Closing on our new property. Right now, we're crashing in my office. The moving company has stowed our furniture until we are ready. Chloe has found a small acreage in Tesuque."

"My partner set her up here since she does all the business real estate," Chloe explained. "I'm the home girl. And the good news is we close in two days. You can call that crew now to build your medicine wheel."

Rachel noticed Chloe used the buzzword, "home," instead of house because it made it sound better. Chloe didn't miss much when finding people houses, er homes, in the City Different.

"I understand you are about to journey to the Land of the Dead," Mari-Lynn changed the subject. "You need protection. I have what you need."

They left the front of the store with its large windows and walked along several rows of immaculate glass shelving. A quick look revealed sage bundles in Native baskets, statues of Kwun Yin the goddess of compassion holding her vessel of tears, Buddha figures, crystal pyramids and candles. But one counter was waist high and contained baskets full of crystals. Each was carefully labeled as to type of crystal and explanation of its benefits.

At the back of the store was a jewelry case. High windows permitted natural light to fill the store. Mirrors behind the counter enhanced the light and caused it to play over the merchandize. Locked inside the glass case were dozens of necklaces, cuffs, malas, and the more precious figurines were protected from bad karma incidents.

Mari-Lynn opened the case and pulled a pendant from the straw scattered in the display for southwest effect. It was in the shape of a pyramid and made of several crystals.

"The top of the pyramid is lodolite, a Shamanic dreamstone used to journey to other worlds and assists communication with higher beings. The Skeleton Man fits this description. Usually only shamans use this stone, but in this case, I think you need it."

Rachel looked at the crystal as it caught the sunshine and reflected light. It was almost as if she could see into another dimension.

"It also protects you from negative energy. You must realize, you likely will be an unwelcome guest." Rachel nodded. “It will also help you move into a meditative state for the vision quest.”

“Lapis lazuli is another protective stone,” Mari-Lynn touched the cobalt blue middle crystal. “It blocks psychic attacks and returns the energy to its source.”

“The largest crystal is blue quartz. It is very powerful. It will adjust its vibrational level to your needs. Most importantly, it is calming if one is fearful.”

This stone was pastel blue, etched with lighter colors of white and cream.

“It comes in many blues from brightest to almost grey; all potent.”

All of the crystals had been cut and polished into flat pieces to fit the pendant.

Mari-Lynn handed the pendant to Rachel. The moment it made contact with her palm, she felt it vibrate. The energy was so strong she could feel it throughout her arm.

“Is it supposed to do that?” Rachel was a bit alarmed.

“That is what you need for a journey such as this,” Mari-Lynn replied. “It will not hurt you, but protect and help you keep your composure under even intense psychic assault.”

“Can you feel it?” Rachel placed it in Chloe’s hand.

“Oh my god, yes,” Chloe said. “This is amazing.”

“How much do I owe you?” Rachel asked.

“Nothing. Chloe has already taken care of that.”

Rachel knew that must mean it was expensive. She turned to Chloe.

“Are you sure?”

“Am I sure I want my best friend protected on a dangerous trip? Yes, I’m sure. It may come into use later as well. You must have it.”

“Thank you,” Rachel said. “And you too Mari-Lynn. I don’t know what we would have done without you. Your crystals have saved us several times.”

“I must add, this particular journey is seldom made,” Mari-Lynn cautioned. “You need to be prepared for the unexpected. We cannot plan for every contingency. I don’t know anyone who has traveled this passageway. I’ve heard of a few who tried, but did not return.”

CHAPTER 22

The ride home was quiet. For Rachel and Chloe the circumstances had become frighteningly real.

"What do you think about doing the vision quest tomorrow?" Chloe asked.

"I think I have to," Rachel said. "With the Dog Star beginning to spiral, there isn't much time.

"I'll call Julian and request a couple of days off, turn in my assignments. May I leave Chile Pod with you?"

"Of course you may. We can snuggle her into the safe room with plenty of her necessities. It's fire proof, has separate ventilation, her own water and AC. It will only be overnight."

"Aren't you going to be there?" Rachel asked.

"I'm not letting you do this alone. I know I can't be right there with you, but I'm going to be close by in case you need help.

"Do your homework tonight and we will plan on the vision quest tomorrow evening," Chloe concluded.

"Okay," Rachel replied. "But in her heart, she knew this wasn't going to be easy."

The following morning, Rachel went to work.

"Morning Rachel dear," Stella said as she came through the vestibule.

"Good morning Stella," Rachel answered. "Is Jules in a good mood today?"

"Uh-oh. Sounds like you need a couple of days off?"

"Can't fool you."

Stella was quiet while Rachel poured hot water, dropped in a tea bag and added stevia. She stirred thoughtfully.

"Good luck dear," Stella said. "I think we may all be depending on your success."

"Thank you Stella. I admit to being somewhat afraid."

"If you were shaking in your boots, you'd have every right," Stella said. "Have you heard the latest on the Dog Star?"

"I guess not," Rachel said with apprehension.

"Cable news is advising everyone to wear masks in case dust from the Dog Star precedes it."

"What?"

"Look around," Stella pointed to the bull pin.

Sure enough, everyone was wearing surgical masks except Stella who was way too cool to succumb to anything so banal.

"What's supposed to be in the dust?" Rachel asked.

"Everything from radiation to stardust," Stella replied with a smile.

"A surgical mask would not protect from radiation," Rachel said.

"Uh-huh. What can I tell you—false sense of security?"

"Okay then, off to see Jules." Rachel took the stairs two at a time.

At Jules office, she tapped on the half-open door.

"Entrée," he bellowed.

"Got a minute?" Rachel asked before sitting down.

"Take a load off." He pointed to the only chair without a stack of folders or mail in it.

"Did you get my assignments?" Rachel asked.

"I did." Jules leaned back in his chair and stroked his beard once. "But somehow I don't think assignments are the only thing you are here about.

"What's the deal with the Dog Star?" He got right to the point.

"It's going to be hard to believe," Rachel began.

"Try me. Remember, I've been around for a couple of your excursions."

"Okay." Rachel took a breath. "I need some time off to take a vision quest and chat with the Skeleton Man in the Land of the Dead."

Jules leaned forward in his chair placing both elbows on his desk. He steepled his fingers.

"Skeleton Man?" His eyebrows tried to meet his hairline. "I see. And it has to do with the ever closer Dog Star I'm assuming?"

"Yes."

"Tell me more," Jules said.

"The Fourth World of the Hopi is about to end, and if it does, we all end with it."

Jules quietly sucked in his breath.

"Doesn't get much worse than that, does it?"

"No Jules, it doesn't."

"Does talking with Skeleton Man buy us more time?"

"That's what I'm going to find out. He may have information we can use to stop the Dog Star. A spirit told me that bad men are desecrating Ancient Puebloan land and that is what put this all in motion."

"Rachel," Julian said. "I know you don't much like being propelled into this role, but for some reason, whether by design or not, you have been. Be careful and *vaya con dios*.

"And so you know I haven't gone soft, have your butt back in the office by the end of the week or I'll send the Jedi to find you," Jules smiled, but it was weak. "Besides I've got you scheduled to cover the Native American parade in the Plaza this weekend."

"I have it on my calendar," Rachel said with forced bravado. "I will be there!"

"But just in case I'm not," Rachel said. "Chile Pod will be at Chloe's. If Chloe's not reachable, please call Dominic. He'll know what to do."

Rachel stood to leave when Stella beeped him on the intercom.

"Jules. Sorry to interrupt. Rachel has a visitor."

"She was just leaving. Get out," he teased.

"Stella," Rachel said. "I'll be right down."

Rachel did a half-halt on the staircase when she saw Anna Cristal and her mother Magdalena waiting in the reception area. Stella had seated them and given a water bottle to each. She was currently squatting and talking to Anna. Stella could talk to anyone.

"Here's Rachel," Stella said to Anna.

Anna jumped up and ran to Rachel, giving her a hug around her knees. Rachel got down and wrapped her arms around her.

"I'm so glad to see you," Rachel said. "No after effects from that trauma in the river?" She looked at Mrs. Cristal

"She seems her old self," Anna's mother said. "But she feels strongly that she needs to talk with you."

"Let's go talk," Rachel showed them the way.

Jules had included a small interview room in the renovations so people could come in. Not everyone is comfortable giving an interview at their house. And some discussions need to be private. Whistleblowers, politicians and shy people often preferred a quiet place off their turf.

Jules had asked the designer to make it comfortable. It was Jules old office so it was at the back of the street level. The walls were a calming blue. A small window looked out at the street. A table stood at one end and seated six comfortably, eight not so comfortably. Stuffed chairs finished out the room; arranged in a semi-circle with a small round table covered in tile so drinks didn't need coasters.

Once everyone was seated, Rachel looked at Anna's mother.

"Are you okay with Anna talking with me?"

"Oh yes, but I should tell you that she has uh, a *gift*," Mrs. Cristal said.

Rachel caught Anna's eye. She appeared to be anxious.

"Would it help if I told you a secret about me?" Rachel asked.

Anna nodded.

"I can speak with spirits and I have a white wolf, also in spirit, who protects me," Rachel said. "The man you saw in the river, I'm fairly certain his name is Joseph. He is in spirit too. The fact that you talked with him tells me you have a similar ability."

"It was Joseph!" Anna declared. "I ask him this time."

"This time?" Rachel asked.

"Yes," Anna said.

"I'm so happy you saw him again," Rachel said.

"Sometimes he appears to me. I knew him when he was alive."

"You know?" Anna said.

"If you mean, do I know about seeing people and animals most people can't see, yes I do.

"Are you happy about the gift?" Rachel asked.

Anna shook her head.

"It scares her," Mrs. Cristal said. "That's why she wanted to see you."

Rachel nodded.

"I'm not happy about having the so-called gift either," she said. "Sometimes I hate it and it scares me." She paused for a moment to think about her words carefully, aware that Anna was a young child. Rachel didn't want to frighten her more.

"I think it's okay to tell spirits to go away if you don't want to talk with them. Spirits are like people in that some are nice and others are not. If you ever see a white wolf with blue eyes, don't be afraid of him. He is a protector of people like us. And I think you know that Joseph is okay. He is a Hopi Indian medicine man or shaman. He is very caring and smart. He won't hurt you either. Anyone you don't want to talk with, just tell them to go away. Okay?"

Rachel looked at Mrs. Cristal to see if she agreed. She smiled, relieved.

"Okay," Anna said.

"What did Joseph want when he visited you?" Rachel asked.

"If I was all right," Anna said.

"That's wonderful," Rachel replied. "He is thoughtful like that."

They all got up to leave.

"Anna," Rachel said. "Go ask Stella for a piece of candy. She has them hidden so the staff won't eat them, but she will give you one."

Anna scurried off, the scariness over.

"Mrs. Cristal," Rachel said. "You might want to read about Crystal Children and psychic aptitude so you have some idea what she is feeling."

"I knew in my heart she did not have Asperger's," Mrs.

Cristal said. "She does have a grandmother who had what was called *second sight*, but she is no longer with us so I can't ask her about it."

"As she grows up, she'll learn what she can and can't do and if she wants to.

"She's a great kid. You should have seen her be brave and grab my hand so I could pull her out of the water."

"I'm so proud of her," Mrs. Cristal said. "With or without the gift."

"I'm not a parent, but I think that's the sign of a good one," Rachel said.

Anna was happily licking a sucker just like any other kid. Stella was fixing one of her braids. Once done, she replaced the rubber band.

"Ready to go honey?" Mrs. Cristal asked. "Let these nice people get back to work."

"I'm available to talk with you or Anna if you feel the need. You can always reach me through the office. Stella even checks in over the weekend. I don't have a cell ... "

"You don't?" Mrs. Cristal was surprised.

"We've decided to call it endearing," Stella said. "Rachel's a holdover from another time."

Everyone laughed, even Rachel, and in a few moments they were gone.

"She like you?" Stella asked.

"Afraid so," Rachel said.

Stella touched her headset and said, "High Desert Country, how can I direct your call?"

Rachel knew it was Chloe because the mutual admiration society commenced. She flew up the stairs and into her office to await the end of pleasantries.

She stared out the window at Mt. Baldy. The aspens were ablaze with color. They were beautiful and yet, there was something off kilter. It must be all the people she could see wearing masks to protect them from what? Radiation? Cosmic dust? The end of the world? It would take more than a flimsy mask to ward off the Dog Star's deadly descent.

CHAPTER 23

Rachel went by home and packed up Chile Pod and her accessories. They would be spending the night with Auntie Chloe in preparation for the vision quest the following evening.

Driving through Santa Fe's narrow streets was a bit like an episode of *The Walking Dead*. It wasn't just the many surgical masks; some wore particulate respirator masks that might actually help filter out damaging chemicals. Everyone seemed dazed and humped over as if they were afraid of something falling on them. And why wouldn't they be? The Dog Star was dangerously close. Rachel could see it spiraling out of control. The Air Force was contemplating shooting it out of the sky. NASA proposed sending a rocket to blow it up. Thus far, no one could decide what the best course of protecting Earth was or if it could be done.

Groups had formed all over the world called "Star Link." Chloe told Rachel #starlink was trending on social media. Members congregated on hilltops, rooftops and in houses of worship contemplating their future and how to cope with whatever was going to happen. Some welcomed the star and others feared for their lives.

Rachel stopped the Merc at a light and waited. At least a dozen people were crossing the street. She absently watched them when a man not wearing a mask turned to look her way. It was Chris!

Instinctively, Rachel started to wave, and then thought better of it. After all, they hadn't seen one another for over a year. He didn't contact her once while in prison nor had he told her about his release. She held still, wanting to say something to him, but what? He was bitter about her role in his arrest. While she could understand why he might think that a betrayal; he shouldn't have gotten involved in illegal activities. She had nothing to do with his god-awful decisions.

Chris turned away and stepped up on the curb disappearing into the crowd. Someone honked behind her. She accelerated with a lurch and continued on her way.

Chile Pod had become accustomed to staying with Chloe. She and Rachel had their own dedicated wing with bedroom, bathroom and office setup. Chile Pod had her food and water under the vanity. Her self-cleaning box was tastefully screened from view with a small room divider in one corner of the bathroom. Every time Chloe invited them over, there was some new accoutrement meant to spoil the Pod Girl—or fluster Rachel, like the exotic shower complete with music, fragrance, color therapy and nozzles spewing water from all directions.

The something new this time was blocking the driveway. Rachel came face to face with a black evil looking iron gate obstructing the entrance to Chloe's property. Rachel hated the things. They were all over Santa Fe, especially in the wealthier areas. She thought about driving around it, but realized that the new gate was securely connected to a new fence. Because no one in Santa Fe wanted to block the views, it was a discerning adaptation of a fence. While certainly sturdy, it was more of a transparent screen painted in a tan color that perfectly fit within the landscape allowing one to see over and through the barrier.

She stopped and visually examined the control box looking for a button to push. It seemed to have a camera, keypad, speaker and slot for a card insert. But where was the damn call button?

"Geez Chile Pod, look what Auntie Chloe has sprung on us this time: a high-tech property entrance? I'm sure everyone in Silicon Valley has one.

She pushed several buttons on the number pad. A screen appeared with an abstract picture of a fountain. It was beautiful as the water rose up, fell and flowed off the edges into a pool below. The water changed colors every few seconds and then the spray pattern would change.

"What the hell?"

"Gee, golly, whiz. Chloe what have you done to me now?"

It would have been relaxing if only it had instructions or some such.

A moment later an ethereal male voice said, "Password incorrect."

"Well, of course it's incorrect," Rachel spoke to the box. "What do you want me to do, Mr. Robot?"

"Please depress the call button," he said calmly.

She began pushing buttons again.

"Which one is the fucking call button?!" Rachel demanded.

"Please depress the call button," it repeated.

"Oh boy, Auntie Chloe's really stepped in it this time," she told Chile Pod who was curious, but understood her human was flustered.

"Please depress the call button." It seemed stuck in a loop.

Rachel tried again.

This time, music filtered out of the speaker: soothing music, of the New Age. She thought it was Yanni, but didn't care.

"Okay," Rachel said. "That's nice, but it doesn't get me in."

"Please depress the call button."

"Rachel?" It was Chloe's voice this time. "Is that you?"

"Hell yes, it's me. Do you want us to stay in the house or out here in the drive?"

"I thought you might have trouble with the gate so I've been watching for you," Chloe said.

"Really?"

"Well, I do have to make an occasional trip to the bathroom," Chloe replied.

The gate began to move to one side. Rachel waited impatiently, pursing her lips in disgust.

Chloe had a garage door open for them when they reached her house. Rachel drove the Merc inside and removed the key as the door closed silently behind them.

"Looks like we made it," she said to Chile Pod. "I'll come around and get you."

Chloe helped them into the house, taking Chile Pod's carrier and releasing her on the floor. After a couple of minutes of cooing, Chloe opened some expensive treats and placed them in Chile Pod's bowl. A bowl that now had the cat's name on it!

"Here," Chloe turned her attention to Rachel. "This is a key card for you. Just slide it into the slot on the gate control and you can get right in."

"Oh, uh, thanks," Rachel said. She closely examined the card as if it might bite, or release nerve gas.

"It doesn't talk, does it?"

"No, only the gate control talks. Didn't the calming image and music make it a more soothing experience?"

Rachel wanted to say something else less ladylike, but went with, "Undoubtedly."

"Okay," Chloe changed the subject. "I've got dinner warming in the oven so let's get some sustenance and then plan tomorrow's vision quest.

"Now, this is the last meal you can have before you proceed with the quest. Tomorrow; only liquids. You have to stay hydrated for the trip."

Rachel hoped dinner was something substantial and not some of Chloe's health food with kale and zucchini she couldn't stomach. Fortunately, Chloe had ordered wisely and a plate of carne adovada, a green chile cheese burrito with pintos and flan followed.

After a satisfying meal and some discussion about the vision quest to come, Rachel and Chile Pod retired to their quarters. Chile jumped on the bed and snuggled into the many pillows. Only her head and tail were visible.

Rachel headed for the bathroom.

"You're lucky you don't have to shower," she told Chile Pod.

With some reluctance, Rachel entered the bath and looked around for something new that would test her IT skills. She settled for a bath instead of the cutting-edge shower. The tub had jets, but she didn't have to use them. A nice relaxing bath sounded heavenly.

Later, with no further technology headaches, Rachel slid

under the duvet into silk sheets. It wouldn't be long before Chloe would have the beds changed to flannel for winter sleeping, but right now Rachel was enjoying the silk. Chile Pod curled up next to her, purring for all she was worth. Rachel slept.

CHAPTER 24

The following afternoon, Rachel and Chloe took Chile Pod to the safe room. Chloe had set up a cat paradise. In addition to the usual necessities for feline rest and nourishment, Chloe had scattered catnip toys and even a small agility course complete with a tube, hoop, A-frame and some weave poles.

"Now for the *pièce de résistance*," Chloe picked up a remote and turned on a screen that had been set into the wall near the floor. "Do you think our Ms. Pod would prefer nature sounds, bird calls or other cats?"

"What?" Rachel said. "I'm not sure what I'm seeing."

"It's streaming for cats," Chloe said with delight. "I'll try nature sounds."

Immediately, Rachel heard a bubbling stream. She looked at the screen and saw falling autumn leaves rustling in a breeze. An occasional rabbit or squirrel walked past.

"Uh, I'm speechless," Rachel said.

"What do you think Ms. Pod?" Chloe asked.

Chile Pod was already swiping at the falling leaves.

"I think she likes it." Chloe beamed with satisfaction.

"Yeah, but what do I do when I get her home and she has no private streaming TV?"

"I have a small one I got for you to use at home." Chloe retrieved it from a counter and showed it to Rachel. It was about eight by five inches complete with a stand to keep it upright.

"Oh, brother," Rachel said.

"Her water and food dispensers are turned on and would

last for three days, but we will be back long before then. Just in case, I've put out extra in old-school bowls."

Chile Pod was thoroughly hugged and made over. Only then, the two women reluctantly left for their expedition.

"I know the perfect spot," Chloe said. "Unless you already have one picked out."

"Haven't given that any thought. I was concentrating on how to actually do the vision quest."

Chloe drove the low road north of Santa Fe leading to the opera, Española and points beyond. Just short of Pojoaque she took the road to Chimayo.

"I know a family here on 503 who have agreed to let us use their property. They have a high hill with some cover, mostly a few piñon and sagebrush to protect from the elements."

Chloe eased the little Lexus into some trees at the base of a hill.

"Will the car be okay here?" Rachel asked.

"Oh sure, the family is nearby. They know it's me.

"Besides, I need the car. I've folded down the two back seats which made a nice area for my sleeping bag, books, lantern and some grub. I can charge my phone in the console and listen to Spa radio all night on my cell. Don't want to run down the car battery."

"Grub, Chloe? Really? I know you must have catered the food."

"You must be hungry and I didn't want it to sound like tasty food. You know, more like chuck wagon food: beans, fried potatoes, coffee with grounds."

"So where do I go for the vision quest?"

"I'll take you," Chloe said. She grabbed half-dozen water bottles from her stash, gave Rachel three and grabbed a tote from her car. They started up a path.

It took about ten minutes to reach the top. The trail would be called moderately difficult in a trail book, but it was short. On the hilltop, Rachel looked about. She could see mountains in all directions. It was a beautiful spot.

"Let's set up a circle for you," Chloe said.

She picked up a stick, stuck the ground to make a center

mark, and then drug the stick in a circle around that mark.

"Now the stones," Chloe said.

Together they gathered rocks and placed them in a circle.

"That looks good," Rachel observed. Now I wait.

"Not in discomfort though," Chloe said. She pulled a blanket and a meditation pillow from the tote. She placed the pillow on the ground and gave Rachel the blanket.

"Keep your water near so you can drink when you need to. I'll be just down the path.

"One more thing," Chloe added. "Here's a whistle if you need anything. It's archaic, but effective."

"You seem to have thought of everything." Rachel was touched that Chloe had put so much thought into her comfort and safety.

"I only want you to concentrate on the ritual," Chloe said. "That will be difficult enough.

"¡Buena suerte!" Chloe wished her luck and disappeared in the dusk as she descended the trail.

Rachel stood facing an incredible New Mexico sunset and wondered what the night might bring. A vision of angry skeletons running towards her suddenly intruded. She shivered.

CHAPTER 25

Rachel sat cross-legged. The meditation cushion made that easy. She drank a bottle of water waiting on, she didn't know what. With the evening chill closing in around her, she had draped the blanket over her shoulders. She had her back to the small grove of aspen and piñon behind her. Looking west, she had a view of the retreating sun. Los Alamos, Bandelier and the Valles Caldera were within her line of vision. Chloe had chosen well. All the actors were aligned where she could see them.

In the dying of the light, Rachel heard something above her. Looking up, an eagle circled over her. She counted three circles and then it flew away. She drained another bottle of water, left the circle to pee and returned. It was colder. Rachel tugged the blanket around her tightly. From a distant hill, coyotes howled in harmony. Some people didn't like the sound, but Rachel found it reassuring. Coyotes were supposed to howl at night. Things were as they should be in some echelon.

There was a cloak of stars overhead. The moon was in the House of Reincarnation that pertained to the cycles of death, rebirth and self-transformation. She didn't know if this was by accident or design.

Wondering about it made her sleepy. Her eyes kept closing and she'd force them back open. It wasn't totally dark because she had the moon and stars in a mostly clear sky and the ever present Dog Star. But looking west, everything appeared normal. She hadn't experienced such gloom many times in her life. She could understand how people could lose their sense of security participating in a vision quest; especially those unaccustomed to total darkness and the wild animals who occupied that mysterious dominion.

She held the pendant tightly, and then rubbed the polished stones. Rachel felt more serene.

Rachel could fight sleep no more. She opened the blanket and crawled in the middle like a sandwich. Careful to stay within the circle, she placed the meditation cushion beneath her head.

"Might as well be comfortable if I can't be warm," she grumbled to the night.

Before she dropped off Rachel reinforced her wish to travel to the Land of the Dead for a solution to stop the Dog Star from impacting Earth. She sent a message to both Joseph and Kiyiya to help if they could.

She slept.

Rachel had no idea how long she had been asleep, but woke to someone nudging her body. Opening her eyes, she saw Kiyiya, the white wolf. It gently pushed at her with its nose. She reached out to touch him but her hand went right through him. She could see him and he could touch her, but she could not stroke him. Disappointed, she sat up.

"What is it? You didn't howl. I must not be in danger."

The wolf turned and looked back at her as if to say, "Come."

Keeping the blanket around her, she stood and followed. But Kiyiya seem to walk off the hilltop into thin air. He looked back again.

This is what *taking a leap of faith* must feel like she thought. He appeared to be asking her to do just that as he stood on nothing, waiting on her.

Rachel, trembling, pushed one foot out into the air, but instead of it chopping through nothing, she felt resistance. She tested by shifting her weight to that foot. It held.

She closed her eyes in an effort to find her resolve, and set the other foot down. It too held.

Kiyiya moved ahead. Rachel assessed each foothold

before moving forward. After a few seconds, it felt normal to walk through atmosphere. She couldn't be sure how long they walked as time didn't seem to be relevant.

The hills of the Española Valley gave way to an ancient landscape. They now walked on familiar ground. The trail was illuminated by four moons. She was not surprised as the number four is sacred to many tribes. It can represent the four directions, colors of mankind, four worlds and other applications.

Two monoliths appeared in the distance. Sinister black clouds roiled at their apex. Thunder crashed. Lightning cracked open the sky and periodically struck the ground. Rachel could feel the impact through her feet. Black and very tall; the towers were formidable. They reminded Rachel of two skyscrapers in a large city reaching high into the heavens only there were no windows. Rachel considered turning around because they ostensibly marked an entrance, but to what? There was a reddish light behind them that she interpreted as otherworldly. It was a color she had never seen before. As she and Kiyiya approached, several orbs of light swirled around them. Rachel speculated they were spirits.

Rachel stopped in awe and not without apprehension. Where had such colossal monuments come from? Kiyiya moved through the opening—or maybe a threshold to an alien land. Rachel followed his glow but was stopped by one of the orbs.

The light stretched up and down from the center of the orb. A translucent spirit appeared and drifted back and forth, deliberately blocking her way.

"You do not belong here," it said. Rachel thought it a female. She could only see the words in her mind as this spirit pushed her aggressively. Although Rachel couldn't see any hands, the impact with her body was firm. She took a step back and tried to protect her torso.

They must have attracted attention because several other orbs floated over to them and their filmy bodies took shape, surrounding her.

"I'm not here to hurt anyone," Rachel tried.

"Why do you come here? Maski is not for the living."

Rachel thought this one to be male. His demeanor felt more threatening. He loomed over her and she could feel pressure on her body from all sides. She was already experiencing difficulty breathing.

"I was summoned by one of you," she managed to say.

"No one would do that," the female specter said.

"Oh yes," Rachel said gasping. She felt as if she'd run all the way. "An Ancient Puebloan came to me and asked me to stop evil men. It is the only way to prevent the end of the Fourth World."

"We do not believe you," another said.

"It's true. I can talk with the dead. I'm doing that right now." Rachel felt an unusual feeling; one of confidence. "He told me to speak with Skeleton Man."

"We welcome the end of the Fourth World," the female said. "Your safe return is of no interest to us."

Rachel's momentary surge of self-belief crashed in a million pieces. She looked for a way out. There were two paths, both poorly lit, but she could see light from the west trail. The east corridor however, was dark with tall cliffs on either side. She heard a cry from that direction, but didn't understand. It would soon become all too clear.

Kiyiya, who had been observing the intimidation of Rachel, arrived silently by the gathering. A low growl followed, but the spirits stubbornly held their ground. Kiyiya was undaunted and tripled his size, and then let go of a high-pitched howl. The spirits became light sources again, but continued to float around her, reluctant to give up their power position.

As Rachel tried to regain her composure, a newly deceased arrived at the entrance just as she had. Two priests emerged from nothing. It was as if they had been there all the time, but she couldn't see them. She recognized them as One Horn and Two Horn priests from the legend of the young Oraibi man. He was the son of the crier chief, or chakmongwi, who was granted a visit to the Maski or Land of the Dead.

She watched as the One Horn priest recited the new arrival's evil deeds that included not sharing food with others, but he had also committed acts of goodness. He had once helped another build a shelter, rescued a child and listened with respect to the elders. He was judged by the two priests and told to take the path to the village where the dead live on.

Rachel understood the two paths now. The next person to arrive was judged. New spirits appeared and began pushing him down the path to a fiery abyss. Flames rose from behind the cliffs and reached out over the road hissing and spraying sparks that rained down on the man and his captors.

"No. No!" he cried. "I helped people. I did."

He tried to fight the apparitions who controlled him, but they were relentless. Screaming, he was thrown into the flames.

"We can easily add you to the deadly glow," the male spirit spoke the words that truly terrified Rachel. She grabbed the pendant and held on for dear life. She tried to prepare herself for what they might do, but how?

A larger sphere materialized. It appeared to speak with Kiyiya. Rachel saw those surrounding her move back a respectful distance. The chatter in her mind stopped. What would this new one have to say? She had a great impulse to run back the way she had come, but that wouldn't save her world. Forward was where she had to go, whatever happened.

The bright sphere concluded its conversation with Kiyiya and approached the orbs that detained her. She braced herself emotionally. But they disappeared.

When the exchange concluded, the sphere approached Rachel.

Again, it stretched and became almost a human. Close enough for her to recognize Joseph.

"Joseph, I'm so happy to see you," Rachel said.

He smiled. She remembered him with great affection and esteem. There he stood in his white pants and belted top. Simple beads adorned his chest. His white hair fell to his waist. She had liked him in life. In death, he had helped her from beyond on several occasions.

"We have verified what you say is true," he smiled. His aura felt more powerful than the others as if he was a leader. But she also felt his compassion.

"You may go west to the village," he said. "Do not stay longer than necessary. If you linger, I cannot save you."

"I won't," Rachel said. She realized her body was shaking.

In a blink of the eye, Joseph was gone.

Rachel joined Kiyiya and together they marched onward quickly through the community where people performed daily tasks of growing crops, making meals and watching children. As they left the thriving town behind, the landscape began to fill in. At first, there was the dry hard ground they walked upon. Then to both sides massive red buttes appeared much as you would find in the Four Corners region of the American southwest. Here, the Mesa Verde cactus grew in abundance. It had become endangered due to poaching and overharvesting. They had entered a different age; a much earlier one.

Kiyiya plodded on, passing numerous turnoffs. If the wolf wasn't guiding her, she would have easily become lost in the forest of agave with their giant spears reaching for the sky. Even though the landscape contained light with no obvious source; it was like a cloudy day at home.

Ahead, the agave gave way to a flat barren plateau. The wolf stopped beside a cliff, lifted his head to Rachel as if to say, *this is it*. He dissolved in a mist. Kiyiya had guided her there; his job done.

Rachel felt abandoned. She was on her own.

A man sat near the rock face. He was elegant and his body intact. Rachel thought he might be a chief. He was an ancient one who wore the horns of the mountain sheep on his head. A white circle enclosed his right eye. He stood as Rachel approached.

"Why have you come?" he asked.

"Is this the Land of the Dead? Maski?" Rachel asked.

"You have reached your destination," he said. "But you do not belong here. You are still strong."

"I know, but I must speak with Skeleton Man," Rachel

said. “It is not my intention to harm anyone.” She’d come all this way and was going to blow it now.

“You have been summoned?” he asked. “You must be summoned to enter or you must be dead.”

Absently, Rachel fingered the crystal pendant Chloe and Mari-Lynn had given her.

The chief’s head turned slightly. He nodded as if he had received a message from beyond.

“You will not harm us,” the chief said. “You are carrying protective stones.” It was a statement not a question.

“Uh, yes.” She showed him the pendant.

“Why do you wish to see Skeleton Man?” the chief asked.

“The Dog Star is falling to Earth. The Fourth World of the Hopi will end if it does. I was visited by a Native from the past asking that I stop it or we will all die. That is why I’m here, to learn how to stop it.”

“Then you will need to talk with Másaw; the one you know as Skeleton Man. He is the Lord of the Dead. He lives in the house you see across the divide.”

Rachel looked at the wide breach between the cliff she was standing on and the house she was trying to see, but smoke blocked the way.

“How do I get there?” she asked.

“First take the sacred corn.” He dropped five kernels of dried yellow corn in her hand. She looked at them not knowing what to do.

“They represent the Five Worlds of the Hopi. Keep them with you,” he said. She dropped them in her pocket.

“Place your blanket on the ground.”

Rachel did as she was told.

“Sit,” he instructed.

She had no idea what was about to happen. Rachel held the pendant tightly in her hand and felt more assured.

The chief waved his arm and the blanket rose from the ground with her on it. Heart in her throat, she soared over the cliff and through sky. She looked about her in the dim daylight, afraid to move. It was a mysterious and miraculous place; one where you could fly. From her magic carpet she could see skeleton children playing on the butte where she was headed. She had anticipated seeing people as only bones, but it was still disturbing. They looked up to watch her land softly on the ground. Not knowing what to do she picked up her blanket and waved to the children.

They were not frightening to her and apparently, she presented only a puzzle to them. They seemed quite interested. One ran over to her and asked what she wanted. Rachel thought it was a young boy.

"I was told that Skeleton Man lived here," she said.

The small skeleton stepped back.

"What is it?" she asked.

"You smell strange," the boy said. "You are living?"

"Yes."

"Then why are you here?" he asked.

"To speak with Skeleton Man," she replied.

"That is Skeleton Woman," the child said pointing to a woman sweeping the ground. The broom looked well-used.

"Thank you," Rachel replied. The child ran off.

She walked over to Skeleton Woman who stopped sweeping but held fast to the broom.

"We heard you were here," she said.

"I'm Rachel. I've come to speak with Skeleton Man, uh, Másaw."

"He is waiting for you; down that road." She pointed.

"Where is the smoke coming from?" Rachel asked.

"You must not go there," Skeleton Woman said. "It is for bad people. Once you go there, you no longer exist.

"Stay on the road to Skeleton Man's house."

Rachel was certain she would do that. She skirted the area where the smoke was coming from and made her way toward the house at the end of the path. More children ran out. One offered her melon. Not wanting to offend, she ate some. It was delicious, unlike any she had ever had. Maybe this was the way it was meant to taste before humankind hybridized it and doused it in chemicals.

"Thank you she said to the skeleton child. It is very good."

They all giggled at her.

"Why do you laugh?" she asked.

The child who gave her the melon said, “We don’t eat, we only inhale the scent or soul of the food. We are lighter than air.” She went on to prove this by floating off the ground a few inches.

“That’s wonderful!” Rachel said. “I wish I could do that.”

She noticed some skeletons in the town were carrying heavy bags of stones.

“Why are they carrying those rocks,” she asked. “Are they building something?”

“No,” the skeleton child said. “They are healing stones. They carry them as punishment for something they did. Soon they can put them down. They will have paid for their wrongdoing.”

“Thank you for the food,” Rachel said. “I must continue to Skeleton Man’s house.”

“You have been called?” A child asked.

“Well, no, not by Skeleton Man, but another spirit person asked me to come,” Rachel explained.

“He does not favor surprise,” the child said.

“I’ll be very careful not to upset him,” Rachel replied, but her body betrayed her by beginning to tremble. Nevertheless she marched onward.

The simple house was located at the edge of the town near another cliff. The wooden structure was primitive and didn’t look like anything she would have conjured in her own mind for the Guardian of the Underworld. She tentatively took the steps and stood at the door about to knock when it swung open.

There was no one there, yet the door opened.

“Hello?” she said.

“Come in,” a deep voice from inside beckoned. “I await you.”

CHAPTER 26

Rachel felt fear creeping along her skin. She visualized the pendant against her chest. Be calm she told herself. This is what you came for. But did she really want to go inside this dark unwelcoming abode?

"You came all this way," the voice said as though reading her thoughts.

Rachel stepped inside the house. Although she had seen the Skeleton Woman and the children, they did not prepare her for what she was looking at now.

"I keep the light away when I have visitors because my remains frighten some," he said.

"I would prefer to see you, if you don't mind." Rachel said hoping she meant it.

Másaw opened the shuttered window and stood before her. It took every ounce of her resolution not to take a step backward and run through the open door. She was surprised to find her hand covering her mouth in shock.

His skeleton was ancient; beyond time. The bones were not bleached white like the others, but discolored by age and abuse, perhaps by physical combat during his human life. Several of his teeth were missing and those left were yellowed. His jaw was twisted. It appeared to have been broken at one time and not healed correctly. When he moved it was not fluid as with the children, his joints creaked and when he spoke his ribs rattled. He was one terrifying entity to gaze upon.

It would have been easy to look away from this former person, but Rachel wanted to reach beyond his appearance. He was after all the Guardian Spirit, Másaw, Lord of the Dead and deserved the respect and honor he was due.

Unlike the others, he was dressed in a breechcloth, a cotton tunic with a leather belt, like Joseph wore. His throat was shrouded in beautiful beads and his head covered with a cloth tied at the side. On his feet were leather moccasins.

"You are not yet ready for this life," he said. "But you were contacted by one of our people?"

"Yes," Rachel agreed. "The Dog Star is threatening Mother Earth. If it strikes us the end of the Fourth World will commence and everyone will die. The man who contacted me said bad men were doing things near Frijoles Canyon and the nearby volcano." She used the name Frijoles because he was more likely to know it than Bandelier.

"I've tried to find out exactly what is being done to the land, but I don't know if I can discover it before the Dog Star hits. Can you help me?"

"I have told my people to live humble lives," Másaw said moving his hands downward as if calming a child. Rachel noticed his knuckles were deformed and wondered if he had arthritis.

"But other people came and have not respected the land," Másaw continued. "Happiness can only be achieved when we live in peace and harmony that includes other people, animals, nature. These people you speak of are not following these laws."

"There are good people too," Rachel said. "Can you tell me how to save the good people?"

"I cannot help you with what the bad people are doing. I do not understand it. But this I know, to stop the end of your world you must prevent the ceremonial dancer from completing his dance."

"What ceremony?" Rachel asked. "Where?"

"It will take place before people who have no understanding or faith," Másaw added. "If the Blue Star dancer removes his mask the Fifth World begins. There is no stopping it."

"That's all you can tell me?" Rachel asked disappointed.

"It is all you need to know," Másaw replied. "Be sure to take your blanket so you can return."

She was dismissed; she turned to go.

"Thank you," Rachel said. "I don't understand it all, but I appreciate that you have spoken with me."

As she turned to go, Másaw spoke once more: " *Kuuyi.*" That was all he said.

CHAPTER 27

Chloe was trying to read in the back of her car, listening to the radio. Unfortunately, she'd read the same paragraph several times. She was worried about Rachel, but hesitated to check on her, fearful it would ruin the journey.

Chloe wished she could have gone along with her, but had never heard of a two-person vision quest. It had been hours since she left Rachel on the hilltop. What was happening?

A light appeared at the rear of the car. Chloe blinked, but it was still there.

"Oh god," she said. "Now what?"

Chloe set down her reader and crawled to the back opening the trunk a couple of inches with the remote. There she saw someone she'd only seen once during their visit to 1940s Los Alamos; Rachel's spirit wolf Kiyiya.

She tried talking with it. "What is it Kiyiya?" Chloe couldn't believe she was speaking with a spirit, someone who protected Rachel.

Kiyiya whined softly; not at all threateningly.

Confused, Chloe didn't know what to do.

Kiyiya turned and trotted toward the path up the hill, stopped and waited.

"Okay," Chloe said. "I'm right behind you."

She followed the white wolf to the top where she found Rachel asleep in the blanket.

Kiyiya nudged Rachel. She wouldn't wake.

Heart in her throat, Chloe shook her sleeping friend.

"Rachel. Rachel!" She heard her name, but couldn't quite wake.

"Rachel!" Chloe said loudly. "Please wake up. You're scaring me."

"What?" Rachel opened her eyes. "Am I back?"

Having done his job, Kiyiya departed.

"I sure hope so," Chloe hugged her. "Did you get to the Land of the Dead? Did you see Skeleton Man?"

"I think so or I dreamed it."

"What happened?" Chloe asked.

"I went on a magic carpet ride."

"Say what?"

"A chief laid my blanket on the ground, I sat on it and he flew me from one cliff to another where the Skeleton Man lived. Some skeleton kids fed me melon and Skeleton Woman gave me directions to Másaw's house."

"Wow, Rachel," Chloe said. "That was quite a trip. But what happened with Skeleton Man?"

"You should have seen him," Rachel said. "He was way past his prime; scary looking guy. He told me that if the Blue Star dancer in some kind of ceremony removes his mask the Fourth World is over."

"What ceremony?" Chloe asked.

"As usual with our kind of sources, he wasn't specific," Rachel replied. "But he added that the dance would be done for an audience of people who had no faith or understanding."

"So, something else we have to figure out," Chloe said.

In the wee hours of the morning, the two friends sat in the frosty air in awe of what had happened. The sunrise was already pushing at the mountains behind them, Rachel told her what she had seen and the strange word Másaw had uttered as she left.

"We'll look it up," Chloe said. "It has to be a clue."

"Let's go. It's freezing," Rachel said.

In the car Chloe asked, "Do you think it was a dream or did you really go?"

"I don't know," Rachel said. "It seemed real, but I suppose it could have been a vision."

Chloe started the car and turned onto the road back to Santa Fe. Rachel dug into her pocket and extracted five corn kernels.

"Chloe," Rachel said excitedly. "Stop a minute!"

Chloe pulled off the deserted road and set the brake.

Rachel held out her hand holding the corn.

"Where did the corn come from?" Chloe asked.

"The Land of the Dead."

CHAPTER 28

Rachel and Chloe grappled with what they had learned. Rachel was tired and hungry. Chloe gave her an energy bar, but it wasn't much of a meal.

At Chloe's house they made over Chile Pod who seemed to not realize she had been abandoned for the night. They found her sacked out in her safe room bed. Some of her food was gone and a few toys had been moved around.

"It was the video," Chloe said. "I knew she would love it."

Rachel wasn't sure about that but she allowed Chloe to have her moment. She had, after all, gone to a lot of trouble and expense to make Chile Pod comfortable and secure.

While Chloe made scrambled eggs and hash browns for Rachel, she heated the green chile she knew Rachel would use to drown her breakfast. Then she turned the soy sausages so everything would be done at the same time. She didn't expect Rachel to eat hers. For herself she made oatmeal and topped it with blueberries and honey. Chloe splurged by adding a little cream.

Rachel sat in the breakfast alcove and called the lab where she'd left the water sample. She listened and made notations in her notebook. Chloe set breakfast on the table and joined her in the nook. Rachel hung up the phone.

"What?" Chloe saw her face.

"The flood water contained high amounts of pumice, sulfuric acid and dissolved iron which is what caused the yellow color," Rachel said. "Here's what I don't understand. They said it was metal-rich and contained mining tailings."

"Mining tailings," Chloe said. "That's bad."

"That's really bad," Rachel said. "They are toxic and have to be kept isolated from the environment or it could be polluted indefinitely. It certainly explains the fish kill."

"I hope the city of Santa Fe is doing what's needed to clean up our drinking water," Chloe said. "It was bad enough when we thought the LANL had contaminated some of our water.

"But there's not supposed to be any mining in that area," Chloe continued. "So what is going on?"

"I have a terrible feeling about this," Rachel said. "I think a return trip to Bandelier is in order. We need to get to the bottom of whatever is going on with the big trucks we saw disappearing into the night."

"Crap," Chloe said. "That doesn't sound like fun, but I think you're right. We have to know what they're doing out there."

Rachel looked down at the plate in front of her. Eggs, potatoes smothered in green chile.

"I didn't know you could cook," Rachel said.

"If you tell anyone, I'll deny it," Chloe retorted.

"This sausage looks suspicious though," Rachel pushed at it with her fork.

"Eat it with green chile and you'll never guess it's soy," Chloe said much as a mother would say to her picky toddler.

"Uh-huh." Rachel took a big bite of her breakfast. "Hey, not bad."

After sustenance, Rachel packed up Chile Pod and headed down the drive, using her gate card without further discussions with the male robot in the box.

"That's better," she said to Chile Pod who only blinked. She had grown accustomed to her person's oddities—like talking to herself.

CHAPTER 29

Rachel took Chile Pod home and got her settled in which consisted of some affordable healthy food that didn't stand up to what she was fed by her Auntie Chloe. It was "thanks mom, but I'll eat that later, much later," a flip of the tail and off she went to sleep away her day on Rachel's bed.

Back in the Merc, Rachel drove to the office.

"Hello stranger," Stella chirped. "Been traveling by broom?"

"Very funny," Rachel replied. "Easier than by dragon." She raised an eyebrow.

"Oh lordy," Stella said. "That's something I don't want to repeat, but it was infinitely better than losing my head to those Dracs."

"It was one wild ride all right," Rachel said. She remembered the escape she and Stella made from Lemuria as it was sinking beneath the Pacific Ocean. Stella had been kidnapped through a painting with supernatural powers. It was the first time Rachel had astral traveled—or ridden a dragon!

"I'm staying away from gallery openings from now on," Stella replied.

"Well, at least stay away from the mysterious artists who do the work."

"Ha! Isn't that all of them?" Stella laughed.

Rachel chuckled as she went up the stairs.

She looked in Julian's office, but it was empty. Rachel wrote him a quick note saying she was doing the fact-checking and final editing on the stories her reporters had turned in.

On impulse she added: "If I'm not in by noon tomorrow,

please call the police. Chloe and I will be investigating at Bandelier. Chile Pod is at Chloe's. If anything goes wrong, call Dominic."

In her office, she compared press releases to the stories she was fact-checking. Made sure that telephone numbers and addresses were correct in the manuscripts and names were spelled correctly. If there was anything the slightest bit controversial, she called the sources and double-checked their quotes. When she was certain they were press-ready, she emailed them to their page designer who would do the layout and coordinate with their printer.

Then she went through the new press releases. Most of the stories in a newspaper or magazine are a result of a request, by way of press release, from organizations or PR firms. A press release is a who, what, where, when, why formula outlining what ballet will be performed, the work of an emerging artist or what's special about an upcoming fundraising festival.

Coverage is everything to arts and nonprofits. Their survival depends on people knowing about them. *High Desert Country* was committed to supporting local arts and causes.

More often, hard news begins in an incident, accident or crime. *High Desert Country* doesn't cover a lot of hard news but monitors police and fire calls. The magazine was designed to cover arts, entertainment, festivals, local news, sports and politics. But Jules said he might want to move into some hard news stories as the magazine garnered more awards and readership. Circulation had increased the past two quarters along with ad sales so it could happen.

She chose stories for the reporters' assignments and emailed a copy of the press release with instructions to the appropriate staff. It was a juggling act. To be editor, one had to remember which stories had been previously published and not repeat them too often. The arts season was year round, but more performances occurred in the colder months. The festivals and outdoor concerts began making their appearance as soon as the weather warmed.

Reporters and editors formed relationships with their regular interviews. A good working relationship could accelerate promotion for their events or issues.

Having completed all her work, she left for home.

Once there, she packed up her hiking gear and the Pod girl. Off they went to Auntie Chloe's. For extra safety she draped the triangle pendant around her neck tucking it behind her shirt.

"Ooh, cold!"

This time Rachel's card got her through the new gate on Chloe's drive without another humiliating encounter with the New Age guy. She did notice the picture today was different: a cairn with the sun dancing on the stones.

When she reached Chloe's house she pulled the car in the garage. The SUV was parked in the drive. Chloe borrowed it again from her partner for their trip.

Chloe greeted them apprehensively.

"What is it?" Rachel placed Chile Pod's cage on the garage floor.

"You didn't notice?" Chloe asked.

"Notice what?"

"Come out here," Chloe said.

They walked out of the garage and looked toward Sandia in the distance.

"See." Chloe pointed to the southern sky.

"Oh my god!" Rachel exclaimed. "You can see the Dog Star during the day now?"She hadn't looked behind her on the short trip to Chloe's.

In the sky a pale spiraling light swirled like a confused cloud. The sight caused Rachel's legs to feel wobbly.

"This is really happening," Rachel said.

"We've got to do whatever is necessary," Chloe said. "Let's get Chile Pod settled into the safe room and be on our way."

This time Chile Pod checked out the food and water, shoved a catnip toy with her foot and climbed in her bed on the floor—facing the kitty entertainment screen. Chloe turned it on and birds began chirping. The tortie closed her eyes. Both women got down on the floor, kissed her head and left.

They retraced the trip to Bandelier they had made earlier. After parking, they began the walk along the trail. They passed their former campsite, but didn't stop. This time, they had only small backpacks with water, energy bars and flashlights.

Chloe had her cell tucked in her bra. On it was a text to 9-1-1. All she had to do was send it, if needed. She didn't tell Rachel.

"I looked up *kuuyi* and it is the Hopi word for water," Rachel said stumbling over a small branch from a nearby tree.

"You okay?" Chloe asked.

"Yup. What do you think about the Hopi word?"

"I think that Másaw wouldn't have said it if it wasn't relevant in some way," Chloe replied. "Maybe he was referring to the flood we had."

"I hope we know soon because, clearly, we don't have much time," Rachel said.

"Perhaps we can learn more tonight."

"Hope so. I think we can get there before dark," Rachel said.

"Good," Chloe answered. "We won't have to use the lights. That would give us away immediately."

As they approached the area where they had watched the truck disappear into the night, they left the trail and walked through the trees. By the time they reached the knoll, it was dark. They crawled the last several yards and watched quietly with only the light from the Dog Star.

For a while all was quiet, but after about thirty minutes, they heard the sound of a truck approaching in the distance.

"We've got to get inside," Rachel said.

"I know," Chloe said. "I was just hoping there was another way."

"Do you want to stay out here? I can go in alone," Rachel said.

"No way you're going alone!"

"Okay," Rachel said. "Let's move down near the entrance and see if we can slip in with one of the trucks."

"I've got a bad feeling about this," Chloe said. "But I also don't have another idea. Let's go."

Carefully they made their way through the shadowy

evening until they were near the entrance. They chose a large boulder to hide behind and awaited the arrival of a truck. Rachel tucked her backpack in the weeds. As a vehicle moved toward them, Rachel noted the truck was dark in color. Faintly she could see letters on the side of the cylinder it pulled.

"Does that say water?" Chloe asked.

"It's hard to tell. The letters look like they've been painted over," Rachel replied.

"I think we could hold onto the back of the truck and get in that way," Chloe observed.

"Okay, that sounds like a plan."

The truck stopped while the driver waited for the opening to appear. Something similar to a garage door began to rise. They heard someone inside say, "Lights!" in a stage whisper. The hidden door rose very quietly. It was a well-oiled door. Rachel thought they must hide it during the day.

"Now!" Chloe said softly.

They scrambled to the back of the truck as the driver pulled into the entry. There was a T-shaped bar to stand on and they clung to a ladder on the rear of the truck that provided access to the hatch on top. The truck sunk into a soft soil as it entered. It felt like the vehicle was going downhill. Once the entire truck was inside, the door closed. Lights came on and people began working. A man spoke to the driver. Rachel and Chloe stepped down and moved to the other side. As the truck moved downward, the two women edged quietly alongside, hoping not to be noticed in the side mirror. When a crevice appeared in the earthen wall large enough to hide them, they slipped inside it and watched as the truck drove a short distance down into the large cavern.

From their vantage point they could see much of the cave. It was large enough to turn a rig around. Once it had, the driver exited the cab. Apparently, all he did was drive because he stood smoking a cigarette while he waited.

"What is this?" Chloe whispered.

"No clue," Rachel replied. "Let's keep a close watch that we aren't discovered."

"Totally get that."

They squeezed back into their hiding place. If they were found, there was no way out. Their attention turned to what was happening below. There was water flowing through the cave. A man with a hose, larger than a fire hose, climbed the ladder on the back of the tank. He opened the hatch and pushed the hose inside.

"Okay," he said.

Water began flowing into the tank. Rachel followed the hose until she saw it was attached to what she could only assume was a pump. The water was coming from below.

"Is that from that an underground stream or part of the aquifer?" Chloe asked.

"My thoughts exactly," Rachel replied. "I'm betting whatever the source, the water is being stolen. Otherwise, there would be no reason for the subterfuge. But why would anyone do it in the first place and what are they doing with it?"

They didn't have time to discuss it further.

"Well, well," a man seemed to materialize out of the dust. Hands on hips he said, "Your husbands' fishing again tonight?"

CHAPTER 30

The formidable looking man spoke to one of his cronies.

"Hey look. These are the dames I saw on the trail the other night."

"How'd they get in?"

"Don't know, but they're here."

"What is this?" Rachel found her voice.

"It's none of your business, that's what," he said.

"Over here," he ordered them. "This way."

He led them downward toward the water while his friend followed them to prevent them from fleeing.

"Is this the aquifer?" Rachel demanded. "Why are you stealing the water?"

"Keep moving." He shoved Rachel but she managed to remain on her feet.

"Back off asshole!" Chloe spit it out.

"Listen bitch, you don't understand. You'd better be saying your prayers. You don't have long to live."

Rachel grabbed his shoulder and faced the burly man.

"You don't understand. None of us have long to live. The Dog Star is going to impact the Earth and we'll all be dead. What you're doing here could be the reason."

Her words did seem to have some effect because he spoke something other than a threat. Everyone had to know about the star plunging toward the planet.

"What's that damn light in the sky got to do with this?"

"Maybe nothing," Chloe said. "Or maybe everything."

"Keep moving," he said. "You can wait on the end of

the world over here." He snickered, shaking his head.

"Are you familiar with the Hopi tribe?" Rachel asked.

"Damn Indians," he snorted. "Got nothing to do with me."

"We are currently in the Fourth World of the Hopi," Rachel attempted to explain. "When the Dog Star hits Earth, it will commence the Fifth World and that means we all die."

"You're crazy," he replied.

"Okay," Rachel said. "Say I am crazy. But all the predictions of the Hopi have come true. All eight of the first signs have come to pass. The Dog Star's descent is the ninth and final sign."

"You two; turn around," he said.

"Search them," he instructed his minion.

The underling didn't seem comfortable with that idea, but he told them to raise their arms.

"Are you kidding me?" Chloe complained. "I've got a tissue in my jeans pocket. That's it."

"Shut up," the boss roared. "Or I'll do the searching and I promise you won't like that."

He obediently patted them down.

"Turn forward," he said gently.

The patting started at their ankles and moved upward. He was about to go bra trawling when Chloe had enough.

"Watch the hands buster!" she warned.

With that, he stopped short of what a TSA body search might have included.

"Now sit down and shut up!" The boss shoved them on the ground near an earthmover sitting idle and left to join the others.

"Look for ways out," Rachel whispered.

"I am," Chloe said. "So far nothing. Since he left us here, I'm assuming he's confident we can't get out.

They sat uncomfortably watching what the men were doing.

"Okay boss," the guy loading the tank said, pulling the hose out of the tank. "It's ready."

The man in charge said to the truck driver, "Get that load to Lea County."

"On my way, Lucas," he said. He crawled into the driver's seat, started the truck.

Someone yelled "Lights" and the cave went pitch dark.

"Let's go!"

Rachel grabbed Chloe's arm and they tried to find their way to the truck using their ears to pinpoint where it was. Chloe hit the earthen wall and stopped.

"We've got to get around the wall into the other chamber," Chloe whispered. "That's the only way out."

They followed the wall with their hands until they got to the end of it and went around. But the door was already closing and all they could see were the tail lights moving away as the door met the ground. The lights returned.

"Where do you think you're going?" Lucas said. "Back where you were."

All night, trucks came and went. When the last truck left, it was obvious that the sun was rising.

"That's the last one," Lucas bellowed to the men. "We need more water for tonight, so get on it."

"Did you hear when he mentioned Lea County?" Rachel asked.

"Yes. Isn't it in the southeastern corner of the state?" Chloe replied.

"Yup. I've been trying to remember why it's significant," Rachel said. "About a year ago, I wrote a story that involved Lea County. There was controversy at the time that New Mexico was buying our own water from Texas for fracking.

"New Mexico has rigid water regulations that apply to both surface and ground water sources," Rachel continued. "In Texas, it's the 'rule of capture.' They can take all the water out of the ground they want, even if the aquifer under Texas is part of the same aquifer beneath New Mexico. Water was being pumped across the state line through hoses just like they're using here."

"Isn't drought a major issue in that part of the state?" Chloe asked.

"Yes, even worse than here," Rachel said. "Apparently there is no law in Texas stating that water can't be sold to New Mexico. As long as the 'owner' of the water is compensated, I guess the powers that be aren't concerned with the perpetuity of their water supply, or ours."

"So they continue to pump water from a shared aquifer," Chloe said. "And now they are stealing water from the Espanola Basin. Water the state depends on to provide drinking water, agriculture and to flush toilets."

"That's about the size of it," Rachel said. "This is why we have to get out of here and report this to the police."

"What are they doing?" Chloe asked, alarmed. "What's that cable for?"

Most of the crew was returning from a part of the cave Rachel and Chloe couldn't see. They all had hardhats on and one man was carrying something that was spinning. Something resembling a cable was rolling off behind him as he walked.

"Oh no," Rachel said. "That's no cable, it's a fuse. They're going to set off an explosion!"

* * *

Julian sat at his desk checking the last minute pages of the magazine before he signed off on them. As usual, there were papers and copies of the magazine covering his desk. He'd noticed several notes that he would get to as soon as he finished this week's proofing. It had priority because it had to be submitted within two hours to be printed by Monday. He glanced down at the date and time on his computer. It was 12:33 p.m. He thought he'd make the deadline.

* * *

"We've got to take cover somewhere," Chloe said.

"Let's get behind the earth mover," Rachel said.

They scooted behind a gigantic tire and looked beneath the beast at what was going on in the main chamber.

No one stopped them this time. Everyone seemed focused on what was happening next. From their vantage point, they watched as most of the men jogged in the direction of the entrance. The detonator was activated.

"Fire in the hole!" Lucas shouted. He and the explosives man ran after the others.

"Get down and cover your ears," Rachel said.

"Maybe we can get out of here after the blast," Chloe said.

Rachel nodded, covered her ears and collapsed on the ground.

Chloe followed but pulled out her cell and sent the text for help to the Santa Fe Police.

The explosion was very loud in the cave and the sound reverberated from one side to another. When it stopped echoing, Rachel let her hands fall from her ears.

"Are your ears okay?" she asked Chloe.

"Can't hear as well," Chloe said. "How about yours?"

"It's coming back. Let's get out of here."

They stopped at the wall that separated the two large caverns and carefully looked around it. The men were yelling and jumping like they'd just seen the Lobos win the Big Dance which would have been a surprise. Just as quickly, they stopped.

The thieves ran to block the water that flowed into the cave. A gate was put in place to capture and hold the water. But suddenly the water stopped. The men looked about, curious as to what was happening.

Rachel and Chloe felt it coming. First a small tremor, then the rumble began. The roar became louder with each second.

"Earthquake!" Chloe said.

"The blast must have set it off," Rachel said looking for a way out.

That's when all the dust and rock belched from the bend in the stream. They only had a few seconds until the cave was filled with choking debris.

"Let's go," Rachel pulled her T-shirt up over her mouth and nose. Chloe used her jacket. They ran for the exit. All hell broke loose. Men yelled incoherently. Everyone was coughing. The door lifted. Light poured in.

Before they could get out, the shaking began in earnest. This time, they weren't 50 miles away, they were near ground zero. The shaking was intense. Chunks of cave's ceiling were collapsing. Dust was everywhere like a thick cloud. Men were yelling out in fear. Lucas was still trying to shout orders as the crew abandoned ship.

Rachel and Chloe, covered in dirt, staggered through the exit to the outside and blinding sunshine. They shaded their eyes with their arms and looked for somewhere to hide. The panicked workers were right behind them. The women did have a head start, but with the moving faults beneath them it was difficult to run. If they hadn't been in such a hurry, they would have seen the earth moving beneath them, pulling apart and pushing back together like a heaving underground ogre.

"There," Chloe pointed. "The clump of aspens."

They ran for the grove leaving behind the backpack and slid inside the canopy. The women braced against the trunk of a tree and waited.

"The earth stopped moving," Rachel observed unnecessarily.

"We'll be missed now." Chloe said.

"Can you climb?" Rachel asked.

"It had to be aspen; no low hanging limbs," Chloe said exasperated.

"I'll give you a leg up; then you can pull me up," Rachel suggested.

"I don't see another way," Chloe answered.

They quickly chose a tree and Rachel boosted Chloe to the first limb.

"Okay," Chloe said doubtfully reaching her arm down to Rachel. "Shinny up the tree."

Rachel grabbed her hand and did her best to *walk* up the tree. At last, she climbed onto a limb breathing hard.

"Aspen aren't the best climbing trees," Chloe said wiping a bloody scrape on her arm.

"Nope, but it's all we have." Rachel had gotten as high as she could and tried to get comfortable while still holding on.

"This is the first place they'll look," Chloe said.

"I agree, but it was the only cover close by," Rachel said.

"I sent a text to the SFPD," Chloe said. "During the chaos before the explosion."

"Good for you," Rachel replied. "Where did you have your cell hidden that Mr. Handsy couldn't find it?"

"In my bra. I thought he was about to go for it, and then he stopped."

"Dammit," Rachel said. "There's no cell service here. Will the text go?"

"Don't know. Had to try it," Chloe said. "Remember after the devastating tsunami in Thailand, most people couldn't call out, but some texts made it through?"

"Good memory."

"We've got company." Chloe pointed at the approaching rag-tag team looking for them.

"We're as high as we can get and not break a limb. Try to look inconspicuous. We don't want them looking up," Rachel said.

"This is your plan?" Chloe whispered.

"I know; it sucks."

With every step their discovery loomed closer. Several of the men had reached the grove carrying various implements of the mining trade.

It was odd, but Rachel remembered someone telling her that aspen grow in a group such as this because they actually support one another through drought by limiting the rate of transpiration. She hoped they would support them now in whatever way possible.

Knowing their location was about to be revealed, Rachel closed her eyes and tried to send a message for assistance to the tree. She was so scared it didn't even seem like an asinine thing to do. The men began to enter the trees. They stopped to allow their eyes to adjust to the shade. Rachel held her breath and kept her grip tight on the limb. She glanced at Chloe who was cool but scared.

A few seconds later, they heard growling from below. Rachel looked down to see Kiyiya. His silhouette barely outlined, she wasn't quite certain he was there but she'd definitely heard the growl.

"Is that?" Chloe whispered.

"Yes."

No one was ready for the aftershock. While they clung to the limbs awaiting certain detection, the aspen began bending and swaying as though blown by an unseen storm. Some of their limbs came uncannily close to the men's heads. They stood in disbelief. It was obvious they didn't want to enter into the grove of turbulent trees, but their fear of Lucas was deeper than their unease of the trees.

"What's going on?" Chloe whispered.

"I think we're getting some assistance from our friends here." Rachel patted the trunk.

Chloe gave her a mystified look.

Two trees at the edge of the grove fell with a crash onto the path of the advancing hunting party, narrowly missing the leaders. They'd had enough. The men ran back the way they'd come.

"What the hell?" Chloe said a death grip on her branch.

"Aftershock."

"Yeah, I get that, but the trees falling at that precise moment?"

"I think we can thank the trees and our lucky spirit wolf," Rachel said. "Let's go, before they decide to try again."

Their intentions were dashed when Lucas walked around the boulder they had hid behind earlier. All the men stopped. He shouted something and pointed with both hands in their direction.

"Find them!" Lucas shouted. "Don't come back without them!"

With sagging shoulders and heads down, they obediently turned and began to fan out in all directions. Four walked back in their direction. Escape was cut off.

***

Mari-Lynn had just packed several crystals and a no fear Buddha in a recycled paper sack with her store's logo on it.

"Thank you," she said. "Here's a schedule of classes coming up soon. Hope to see you then."

The customer thanked her and left the store happy. But Mari-Lynn was not happy. She had a bad feeling. In the lounge area of the store, a heavy-hearted, she sat in a chair and closed her eyes.

Why was she seeing trees? Both hands went to her temples. She was having some pain there. It must be bad she thought. Mari-Lynn focused on the vision she was receiving. This time it was a barren area, but there was a grove of aspen in view. In her mind, she flew above the land. Near the trees were men, angry men, looking for something. They carried sticks, picks and one had a gun. She glimpsed what looked like a white wolf and trees falling which seemed to frighten the mob. In an instant, she flew closer, hovered over the grove of aspen. When she had maneuvered directly over the trees, she raised both hands in a parting gesture and watched as the leaf canopy opened for her. There, clinging to the upper branches were Rachel and Chloe. Their faces wore fear.

CHAPTER 31

Mari-Lynn was calm in her dream state, but her mind registered her friends were in trouble; maybe serious trouble. She rose in flight to a greater height. Where were they? She could see small groups of men fanning out. Some had tools pounding the desert scrubs, combing the arroyos and looking behind boulders. As Mari-Lynn piloted higher she saw they were near Bandelier.

"Oh my god," she momentarily came out of the trance. "That's where the university men were found dead." Her friends were in jeopardy and needed help immediately.

* * *

At the 9-1-1 center a strange text had been received. The manager patched a call through to the Santa Fe Police Department.

"Dispatch." The officer said.

"This is the floor manager at 9-1-1," she said. "We received a text. I'm afraid it's gibberish, but here's the number. We traced it to a general location but couldn't pinpoint. It's in the Bandelier area."

"Oh man," the dispatcher said. "That's 33,000 acres! Can you be any more specific?"

"We think it's on the Valles Caldera side. An earthquake occurred there just a few minutes ago so it could be a hiker who was injured from falling rock."

"Okay," he said. "We'll alert Los Alamos PD and see how they want to proceed. Thank you."

"Good luck." The 9-1-1 manager had one of those feelings she got when a distress call that wasn't a straight-forward call for help. She sent out a hurried prayer and went on to the next call. They had done all they could.

"Hey, I have another call about Bandelier," one of her operators called out.

"The caller said she knows exactly where two endangered women are," the operator said.

"Only one thing."

"What?" the manager asked.

"She said she had some kind of vision."

"Let me talk to her," the manager plugged in her headset. She identified herself and listened. The woman didn't sound like a kook and they had nothing to go on but her information. It didn't sound like a hiking accident at all, but the women were in great peril. She thanked her and called Los Alamos PD herself. At least they'd have a starting point.

When the Los Alamos PD answered she said, "You won't believe this, but I do."

* * *

Mari-Lynn hung up the phone and greeted her customer, but she remained concerned. When she was once again alone in the store she checked her local news feed; still no word on a rescue of two women. Although there was nothing left she could do, she couldn't help but worry. Her visions could show her what was happening, but she had no control over events as they unfolded.

* * *

Stella heard the door open, but at first didn't see anyone.

"Mrs. Dallas," Anna said barely able to see above the pony wall that separated the reception area from her work space.

"Hello Anna," Stella said as Anna's mother followed. "How can I help you today?"

"May I leave a message for Rachel's, uh ... ?"

"Her supervisor," Mrs. Cristal completed the sentence for her.

Anna nodded.

"Of course," Stella said with pen poised above pad. "What is it?"

"A friend of Rachel's—his name is Joseph—told me that Rachel is in danger."

"Hang on," Stella pushed Julian's intercom.

"Yeah Stella," Julian said.

"Rachel's friend Anna is here and she said Joseph told her Rachel is in danger."

"Rachel left him a message," Anna said pulling herself up as high as she could to see Stella.

"Did you hear that?" Stella asked Julian.

She could hear rustling as Julian went through the mound of papers on his desk.

"He's looking," Stella said.

"Oh damn!" Stella could hear Julian say. "It's here. I've got to call the police. Thanks Stella."

Julian called 9-1-1.

"This is Julian Brazos, publisher of *High Desert Country*. One of my reporters may be in danger."

"Do you know where the reporter is?" a woman asked.

"She's at Bandelier with a friend. She left me a note saying to call for help if she wasn't in by 12:30 today. Oh god," Julian cupped his head with his hand. "It's 2:15!"

"Just a moment," the dispatcher said.

"Mr. Brazos, this is Eleanor Torres, dispatch manager. We've already received a call and a text regarding these women. I've notified Los Alamos PD and they are responding. Are these people reporters?"

"Rachel Blackstone is my reporter and Chloe Valdez is a friend."

"Is your reporter on assignment?"

"Yes," Julian said. "She's investigating the earthquakes occurring in the area of Bandelier." That's all he could comfortably say without lying or giving away Rachel's true mission.

"We've identified the cell number that sent the text as belonging to a C. Valdez," Eleanor said.

"They may have run onto some illegal activity in that area," Julian added. "They could be in danger. I don't always know what a reporter will find."

"Okay, Mr. Brazos. I'll alert the Los Alamos PD to that."

Julian hung up the phone; rubbing his temples.

"Oh god, I hope she's not in over her head this time."

His intercom buzzed.

"Julian," Stella said. "Call for you from Dominic Magellan. Says it's about Rachel."

"Thanks Stella."

"This is Julian."

"Dominic Magellan, do you remember me?"

"Yes. You're a friend of Rachel's."

"Listen, I don't want to start a panic or anything, but I haven't heard from her and I've given her a couple of hours to report in. Can't reach Chloe either. Miss Chile Pod is at Chloe's house. Should I go get her? And do we need to call the police?"

"The police have been called and are in route. As to Rachel's kitty, yes, I think you should go get her until we know what's going on.

"Do you have keys to get in Chloe's house?"

"Yes," Dominic answered. "I've got both Chloe's and Rachel's keys in case of emergency."

"Are you in the loop as to what Rachel is specifically trying to do?" Julian asked.

"The gist is that Rachel's trying to stop the end of the Fourth World of the Hopi. That's why the Dog Star is getting so close. Rachel's trying to discover what's going on near Bandelier that's causing the earthquakes. If she can find out, we may all get to live a little longer."

"Okay," Julian said. "You take care of her cat. She would be worried about her. And I'll head out to Bandelier.

"Thanks Dominic."

"And you." Dominic rang off.

He pocketed his cell and glanced out the window. The Dog Star was fully visible in the daylight sky. He hoped Rachel could solve the mystery in time.

Julian raced down the stairs to reception.

He stopped for a moment and took Anna's hand.

"Thank you," Julian said. "Thank you for coming here and helping Rachel."

Anna looked up at the tall man with the beard and nodded.

"Stella, I'm going out to Bandelier. Send everyone home early. And if you say prayers, it might be a good time."

Stella crossed herself.

"Julian, be careful. Bring our Rachel back."

CHAPTER 32

Rachel and Chloe were still clutching tree branches when another aftershock hit. It felt more powerful than the first.

"Aren't they supposed to diminish in magnitude?" Chloe had to yell to be heard.

"That's the way it generally works," Rachel said. "We've got to get out of here and back to the car."

"Are they still searching?" Chloe was sitting one direction and Rachel the other to keep watch.

"They're all huddled together right now," Rachel said. "I think the aftershocks are unnerving them."

"They sure as hell are me," Chloe said. "But if we make a break for it, someone will see us. Rachel, I'm afraid they will kill us like they did those men from the university."

"I know, but we may have bigger problems," Rachel said.

"How could we possibly ... ? Chloe trailed off.

"Do you feel it?" Rachel asked.

"Yes." Chloe looked at her friend. "Another earthquake?"

"I'm not sure. I feel sensations from the ground coming right up the trunk of this tree."

"We need help," Rachel said. "I'm calling in reinforcements."

Rachel pulled the pendant out of her T-shirt and held it in her palm. Trying to ignore the pulsating she continued to feel through her body, she went inside herself and called on Joseph.

I think you're on a vocal fast from me, but we need help. Can you help us?

A few seconds later, there was a thunderous blast to the west of them. It sounded like more explosives had been set off.

"All those guys are out here looking for us," Chloe said. "Who's detonating dynamite?"

"I don't think it's dynamite," Rachel said. "Do you smell that?"

Chloe wrinkled her nose.

"Yes, smoke and what?"

"I think volcanoes discharge sulfur among other bad stuff," Rachel added.

The smell of sulfur hung lightly in the air.

"Can't miss the rotten eggs smell and it's not good," Chloe said.

"No," Rachel said. "I hope it doesn't get any stronger. It can kill."

"I've called on Joseph for help, but the time may have come where we take our chances with those men. They may be as afraid as we are."

"Even if we get back to the car," Chloe said. "If we're talking a supervolcano explosion, we're all toast."

Rachel started to answer when she heard the growl below.

"Kiyiya," Rachel pointed at the ground. "Come on, get down. This is our chance."

Once on the ground the white wolf in spirit began moving away from them. But he stopped and looked back.

"Come on," Rachel said. "He wants us to follow."

Touch the wolf. Joseph pressed into her thoughts. *His invisibility will shield you.*

"We're supposed to touch the wolf," Rachel said. "Joseph says he will hide us. But I tried to pet him the other day and couldn't."

Rachel reached for his back and found she could touch him now.

"Go ahead," she said to Chloe.

Chloe followed, first with just her index finger.

"He's so soft," she said.

"Isn't he?" Rachel said.

Walk with him to safety. Joseph intervened once more.

"We're to walk with Kiyiya to safety," Rachel said. "That would be those trees."

"Okay," Chloe said with some distrust. "He will really keep us invisible?"

"Straight from Joseph," Rachel said. "We have to believe."

Slowly at first, they ventured from the small aspen grove and walked into the clearing that separated one group of trees from another. Rachel looked back. Only an angry Lucas holding a gun was looking their way searching for any movement. The other men were disbanding to wherever their vehicles were to make a hasty trip home.

"Don't let go," Rachel cautioned.

"No way I'm letting go," Chloe said.

"Do you think that the Valles Caldera is really going to go off, big time?" Chloe asked.

Rachel didn't answer, just looked at her friend. They both knew this could end badly, but neither could say so out loud.

They were so close to the forest when Chloe tripped over a branch lying on the ground. Momentarily, she appeared alone in the clearing. Lucas saw her. He started running their direction.

"Oh damn," Chloe cried out.

"Quick," Rachel said. "Grab hold of the wolf."

Chloe grabbed a handful of Kiyiya's ruff and disappeared again.

Lucas continued to run in their direction even though he could no longer see Chloe.

The trio reached the forest. Once inside, they looked back. Lucas approached the trees.

"He's coming in," Chloe said. "What do we do?"

"Get off the trail, get down and continue to hold onto Kiyiya." They both squatted, one on each side of the wolf.

Kiyiya stood silently guarding his charges, allowing them to hold onto his body. This was what he had been chosen for; to protect Rachel and now her friend.

Lucas burst into the trees brandishing the gun. He was

livid, Rachel was afraid he would start shooting despite not seeing them. He turned in all directions.

"I know you're in here! Don't think I'm letting a couple of bitches get away."

It was all bravado. Moments later the ground began to rumble again. Sulfur and smoke belched from the caldera. Lucas ran.

When he was out of sight, Rachel and Chloe stood up. Kiyiya, having done his job didn't stay around for thanks.

The two made good time on the trail. In the open they could see the smoke lifting into the sky from the caldera.

Rachel could feel the adrenalin continue to pump. Her mind raced with thoughts of a huge hunk of New Mexico just vanishing.

"Look Rachel," Chloe pointed a group of men and women rescuers congregating at their car.

One police officer approached.

"Are you the women who needed help?" he asked. "We got a text message and several calls alerting us to search."

"Wow, the text message got through?" Chloe asked.

"We were told it was garbled, but they could read your number. Is this you?" He held up his cell showing her number and jumbled text.

"Yes," Chloe answered.

"Are you both alright?"

Rachel told the police who formed part of the group what they had discovered. The water poaching operation, the explosions, how they had been captured and could have died in the process. How the men had chased them and given up due to the eruptions. She carefully left out the white spirit wolf who had protected them.

The medics checked them out and approved their departure. The firefighters gave them directions for the safest route out of the area as roadblocks had been set up to prevent gawkers and avoid injuries or deaths should the volcano blow.

When they were finally on the way home, Chloe said, "We did it. We found the evil men and the authorities will stop them from pilfering any more water."

"If they can round up all of them," Rachel said doubtfully. "I'm sure they're New Mexico's best at becoming invisible."

"Still, it's stopped," Chloe replied.

Sandia Peak came into view.

"No," Chloe said. "That's not possible."

Rachel looked at the southern sky and saw that the Dog Star was as menacing as ever.

"Rachel, it's still there!"

Rachel pulled over and they got out. It was a perfect azure sky with the exception of the smoke behind them. Chloe was right, Sirius was still there and it looked even closer.

"But we've found the evil men and turned them in," Chloe said. "Why is it still coming?"

Rachel squinted as she studied the spiraling star.

"It's not over."

CHAPTER 33

Santa Fe's Plaza was a blur of people. Most were wearing masks. Light smoke was noticeable with no identifiable source. There was a street preacher shouting that the end of the world was at hand. Some people clustered together and spoke nervously starring at the sky. Others hurried here and there with no apparent destination. Every face displayed fear or confusion. Could panic be far behind? A few determined tourists sat on the benches of the Plaza pretending to relax but looked like they were ready to sprint at a moment's notice.

Chloe's phone sounded. It is illegal to use a cell while driving in Santa Fe so she handed the phone to Rachel.

"Would you look and see what it is?"

"A text from Dominic. He picked up Chile Pod at Julian's urging."

Chloe guided the SUV around and out of the Plaza to take Rachel to Dominic's house.

"Geez, that crowd is some scary stuff," Rachel said.

"If this is not over, and it doesn't look as though it is," Chloe said. "Remember, you and Chile Pod have a permanent invite to my safe room."

"Thanks Chloe. We'll keep that in mind."

"Seriously, I have gas masks, iodine and MREs. Along with water in the storage closet you haven't seen yet," Chloe paused for a breath. "And enough medical supplies to do surgery if we had to. We could hide out for a couple of months and wait for the fallout to cease or the sulfur to clear."

"Chloe!" Rachel looked at her friend in amazement.

"I had the safe room built right after that Jodie Foster movie came out called *Panic Room*. You know the one where the tough guys break in to their New York City house. She and her daughter hide in their safe room, but she couldn't get to the insulin in time and her daughter has to have it," she ended breathlessly.

"Uh-huh," Rachel absently.

"There is a small bathroom with shower and toilet. Bunk beds for sleeping and you've seen the kitchenette. We could hole up real cozy."

Chloe had been talking so much Rachel didn't realize they had arrived at Dominic's house. She pulled into the small horizontal parking spot and shut off the car.

Inside, Juan was working on some new burglar-barking, but as soon as he saw Rachel and Chloe it all stopped and he went over for some attention. Rachel looked around, but didn't see Chile Pod.

"Oh, our girl is in her room." Dominic led the way to the room with the big window, a cat's dream because of the view of the bird bath and feeders. At this moment a squirrel was partaking of the bird seed. But Rachel still didn't see her cat.

"We've added something new," Dominic said. "Juan and I went to the pet store and picked out a cat tree for the Pod's visits."

"How thoughtful of you," Rachel said hugging Dominic. "Thank you for looking after her."

Sure enough, in one corner by the window, the tortie had a front row seat to anything going on in the backyard. She was happily half-napping in the top spot. It was easily five-feet tall with three levels to nap.

"Hey Pod," Rachel said reaching to pet her. She raised a sleepy face to get some rubbing.

"Okay, you're happy. I'm going to go talk with Auntie Chloe and Dominic."

By the time she returned to the dining room, slash, office, Dominic had gotten them all beers and some cheese and crackers to munch on.

"Oh thank you, Dominic," Rachel said. "I'm so hungry."

She inhaled a couple of crackers and a slice of cheese.

"You're welcome. Sit."

"Chloe's been telling me the short version. I'm very glad you both survived."

"May I use your phone?" Rachel asked Dominic.

He handed her his cell. She dialed the office, listened to the answering service.

"That's odd," Rachel said. "The office is closed." She texted Julian instead letting him know they were okay.

Before they could say another word, Dominic's phone rang. "It's Julian." He handed Rachel the phone.

"Julian. Where are you? Why is the office closed?"

"I went looking for you. Got your note. Are you both okay?"

"Yes, but it was close," Rachel said. "We managed to hike back to the car where some EMTs and firefighters met us. They told us how to get out of the area. We're at Dominic's now."

"Thank god. I was afraid you'd gotten in over your head."

"Oh, we were in over our heads all right, but we had a little help," Rachel replied.

"I'll take that to mean not of this world," Julian said.

"You could say that," Rachel said. "How did you know we were in a bit of trouble?"

"Your friend Anna came to the office and told us you were in danger. And only then, did I find your note.

"But I couldn't get through by car. There's a roadblock near Espanola. I closed the office because I didn't know what might happen next. There are people stopped along the highway gazing at the sky. It's eerie."

"We're okay," Rachel said. "I'll see you at the office tomorrow."

"Is there going to be a tomorrow?"

"With any luck," Rachel answered. She returned Dominic's phone.

He took a swallow of beer and said, "Did you see Skeleton Man?"

"Yes," Rachel replied. "It was all very strange and frightening."

Rachel caught up Dominic on her visit to the Land of the Dead.

"You've identified the bad guys," Dominic said. "Why is the Dog Star still threatening to take us out?"

"Something Skeleton Man said is nagging at me," Rachel said. "As I left he said *kuuyi*."

"What?" Dominic asked."

"I'm sure my pronunciation is wonky, but it means water," Rachel said.

"That would make sense," Chloe chimed in. "Those jerks were stealing water from an aquifer and apparently transporting it to the southeast corner of the state to use for fracking."

"Did he say anything else?" Dominic asked.

"Yes, but it's confusing," Rachel said. "The spirit who visited me after the bird kill only spoke about stopping the evil men. It seems that we have done that, although they're surely not all arrested yet. But Skeleton Man told me a story about a dancer. He said if the dancer removes his mask during the ceremony, the end of the Fourth World begins."

"But, no specifics?" Dominic asked. "Like who or where or what ceremony? That could be so many places in the Southwest."

"That's just it. I don't know. He wasn't much for particulars. Frankly, I wanted out of that creepy ghost house and as far away from that moldering Skeleton Man as possible."

"So that leaves us with another mystery to solve." Chloe said with resignation.

"It does." Rachel sighed.

"There is a story from Hopi culture that might shed some light on this," Dominic said. "The Hopi Prophecy Rock in Oraibi, Arizona foretold two great earthquakes. Here's a photo of the petroglyph."

Rachel and Chloe leaned across the table as Dominic pushed an open book toward them.

"The large figure on the left represents the Great Spirit," Dominic said. "These four smaller figures symbolize the Four Worlds. They are located on the Path of Life. The two circles are the great 'earthquakes.' This smaller circle indicates the last chance to return to the sacred life before the Great Purification.

"Some historians of Hopi storytelling have interpreted the earthquakes as WWI and WWII. We could interpret them as the two actual quakes that we've received here in Santa Fe."

"Say we do construe it that way," Chloe said. "What is next?"

"The Day of Purification," Dominic replied. "In most cultures there is a great flood story. The Hopi are no different. After their devastating flood, the survivors and the Great Spirit made a covenant that was written on a set of sacred stone tablets called Tiponi. It contained his teachings, but also prophecies and perhaps most importantly warnings of how things should be. The people were to protect the land until the Great Spirit returned. They settled in what we now call the Four Corners and what they call the heart of Turtle Island or the U.S. There they would live in peace and wait for the return."

"Unfortunately," Rachel said. "That means the end of our civilization?"

"I'm afraid it does," Dominic said. "The prophecy states that WWIII will commence when the people who first received the Light initiate war. I can only tell you what I've studied and I emphasize this is an interpretation. The countries named included Africa, Palestine, India and China. And the prediction is the U.S. will be destroyed."

"That's comforting," Chloe said. "Anything else?"

"Nothing good, but yes, there is a lot more, but this stands out to me," Dominic said. "Turtle Island could be flipped on its axis, which some researchers say could be a pole shift. The Hopi call this world off its balance the *Koyaanisqatsi*. Worst-case scenario, cold regions would become hot and food crops would fail leading to mass starvation. This would call for a new direction, one more respectful of nature and each other."

"It boils down to this," Rachel said. "How do we stop it?"

CHAPTER 34

Anna woke in her room in the predawn hours. She wasn't alone. This had been happening more and more frequently. She remembered what Rachel told her; she didn't have to talk with spirits if she didn't want to.

"Go away," she said to the darkness. "I want to sleep."

"It is Joseph," the spirit said. "Could you spare me a few moments?"

Anna sat up in bed. There was Joseph at the foot of her bed dressed in his familiar white garments cinched at the waist, long silver hair falling down his back.

"What do you want?" she asked somewhat annoyed at being pulled from sleep once again.

"I have information for Rachel," Joseph said.

"Can't you just tell her?" Anna whined.

"You are a promising medicine woman. I am helping you learn."

"Did you help Rachel when she was little?" Anna asked.

"Yes, but she did not know it," Joseph replied. "She resisted guidance as a youngster; much like you," he smiled remembering. "Rachel still resists, but she is becoming a good sensitive. But I couldn't reach her when she was a child.

"Are you willing to try?" Joseph asked.

"Okay," Anna said sleepily.

"Remind Rachel of the cats-ee-nah." There was that word again. "Mother Earth is in pain. The dead birds, earthquakes and floods are Her wailing for help. Will you tell Rachel this?"

"Yes," Anna said.

"I bid you goodnight." Joseph faded away.

The following morning, Anna wasn't sure if she had dreamed it or if Joseph had really paid her a visit. Despite her uncertainty, Anna asked her mother to call Rachel at work.

Rachel was at her desk reading press releases and assigning stories to the other writers when Stella buzzed her.

"Hey Stella. What's up?"

"Your young friend Anna wants to talk with you," Stella replied.

"Put her through. Thank you."

"Hi Anna. This is Rachel."

"I think Joseph talked to me last night," Anna said.

"But you're not sure?"

"No. I was sleeping."

"Even if you dreamed it, he may have still have visited. What did he say?" Rachel asked.

"He said to remember it's the cats-ee-nah and Mother Earth is in pain," Anna replied.

"Did he explain about the cats-ee-nah?" Rachel asked.

"No."

Rachel sensed that Anna was tiring of what she might consider a game.

"Thank you for telling me. I'll take it from here. You can tell Joseph if you don't want to do this."

"I want too; but tired," Anna said.

"You may also feel like it's too much right now," Rachel answered. "That's okay."

Rachel didn't want Anna to feel overwhelmed. After all, she was a small child. This psychic stuff was often more than Rachel wanted to deal with too.

"Maybe you should spend part of your day playing outside," Rachel suggested. "Take some time away from this adult stuff. Okay?"

"Okay," Anna said. "Bye."

"Bye Anna."

Rachel turned in her chair to look at the mountains. She was thoughtful as she considered what Anna told her. She could see how Mother Earth was suffering.

She picked up a press release on the festival of Native

American dancers that would be in town over the weekend. She was doing the interview tomorrow with their spokesperson and was looking forward to that despite the heaviness of the current situation. Tribes were coming from all over the Four Corners. She hoped the Plaza would be packed with people learning more about the culture in spite of the uncertainty.

She glanced at the clock on her desk. Time had flown as she made assignments and researched her upcoming stories with the constant background of thoughts pounding in her mind. This mystery wasn't over yet.

CHAPTER 35

The howl of the wolf echoed across the city. Rachel woke to find her face wet. Her tortie cat sat on her chest licking her chin with urgency. The TV she left on played soft music that helped her sleep. It changed quickly as a shrill noise from the television drowned out the music. When she exhaled, fog formed in front of her. She shivered.

Rachel gently picked up the cat and held her defensively. Chile Pod didn't object. She had experienced this before. Disturbances weren't exactly new, but not common place either. And they rarely occurred inside the house.

Rachel stood and gently shoved Chile Pod under her bed.

"Stay," she said. "Please stay."

She wrapped up in her robe and went into the living room. Rachel was not alone, but whatever it was hadn't put in an appearance yet. Maybe she should allow Chloe to heighten her security system, but would it work against spiritual intruders? Her blood pumped at high-speed, her neck prickled and despite the cold, a trickle of perspiration ran down her back.

She thought it must be a spirit, but usually it didn't take long for them to appear. Rachel turned taking in the whole room. Nothing but her comfortable living room, kiva fireplace in the corner with a pile of ashes that needed to be removed, comfy sofa she and Chile Pod loved to nap on, the stack of work on the coffee table she'd brought home and not done.

"You're really taking your time," she muttered.

The TV went silent; the cold increased.

"Show yourself," Rachel demanded. "Why are you hiding?" It sounded brave. She wasn't. Rachel's grounding in journalism was based on facts. Her new identity as intuitive ran contrary to her training. And damn, if she didn't seem destined to continue in this vein.

Rigid with dread, she waited, glancing about the room cautiously.

"Come on," she demanded. "Let's get the show on the road."

Light flashed several feet in front of her. It looked to be in human form, but kept coming in and out like bad special effects in a sci-fi movie.

The rattling sounds commenced and became quite loud. It seemed to give the spirit the courage to slowly appear; first its bare feet and then his full body. It was the Native man who first warned her about the evil men.

"You have done well thus far," he said.

"What do you mean?" Rachel asked.

"You have found the servile ones; not the leaders," he said. "They will only begin again. They are taking the lifeblood from Mother Earth."

"Tell me where these leaders are and I will turn them into the authorities," Rachel said.

"One is nearby," he said.

"Who?"

"I know not his name," he said.

"Look closely," he replied. "The Dog Star will continue its descent if you do not find the source. It will be soon; matter of days."

"Oh, for heaven's sake," Rachel was exasperated. "Why can't you just tell me?"

"I am told he is close to you. You will find him."

That was followed by a sucking sound as his image became vapor and dissipated.

"Well, that's just great!" Rachel said angrily with a stomp of her foot.

The TV screen once again showed video. She switched the channel to an overnight news channel and plopped on the sofa. Chile Pod looked around the door to the bedroom with big green questioning eyes. Her person had some weird visitors, but it interrupted the boredom of napping and eating.

"Come on sweetie," Rachel said. "Jump up." She patted the sofa beside her.

"You're just what I need," Rachel said and scratched her head. Chile Pod moved her head around depending on where it itched.

The cable news anchor droned on about current politics and the price of health care. She then reported a soft news respite concerning the recent births of pandas in China. Rachel was about to turn it off when something of interest caught her attention.

Scientists say if a solution can't be found, Sirius, the Dog Star, may collide with Earth in a matter of days.

As she spoke, footage of the star at various stages of its approach ran, followed by meetings showing men and women discussing the situation around an oval table. A screen on the wall depicted possible resolutions.

NASA has their top scientists working on a solution that could involve destroying the star while in space or changing its trajectory. No one seems to have an explanation for the star's behavior, but there is a consensus that if it hits the planet it could have an apocalyptic result not seen since the dinosaur extinction.

This was followed by another expert who said it was too late to do anything, but pray.

People in the U.S. and around the world who have the means to do so are moving to underground bunkers in secret locations. Looting has broken out in some cities as people try to hoard food, water and medical supplies.

There were several scenes of people breaking store windows and fleeing with essentials, giant packages of toilet paper and boxes of diapers. Some carried large flat screens and computers.

Officials request the public remain calm and prepare in legal ways. We will continue to keep you updated on this fast-moving story.

With that, she moved back into politics as if the world wasn't ending; even patting her hairdo that was sprayed stiff and afraid to move.

Rachel had been so involved trying to stop the Dog Star in its tracks that she had missed several newscasts. Before she could think about it more, her phone rang.

"That has to be Auntie Chloe," Rachel said as she left Chile Pod purring on the sofa.

"Hello Chloe." Rachel didn't even glance at the caller ID.

"Something woke me and I felt like you needed me. Are you okay?"

"Are you becoming psychic too?" Rachel asked.

"Oh, I hope so!"

Rachel told her friend about the past few minutes including the coverage on cable news.

"How do we find out who this person is?"

"The spirit said he was close, so we've got to stay vigilant and suspect everyone. I'm doing an interview this morning with the executive director of the Native American festival happening in the Plaza tomorrow afternoon. We've already done a preview story so this goes on our website update page. After that, we can get together and somehow find this guy."

"So we just act normal instead of running through the Plaza screaming the end is near?" Chloe asked.

"Yeah, normal," Rachel said trying to make it funny and failing miserably. "Otherwise, we're so screwed."

CHAPTER 36

The executive director for the Native American dance festival was normally in her office in Albuquerque, but today she was in the *High Desert Country* offices while in town preparing for the festival. Rachel could see her and a companion in the interview room. She greeted Stella and picked up messages.

"Good morning," Rachel said as she entered the room.

"Hello Rachel," Octavia Chavis, executive director of the Four Corners Art Consortium. "How nice to see you again."

Octavia was dressed in a conservative navy suit. Her grey hair was pulled back in a lovely chignon. She was always elegant and one of Rachel's regular interviews.

"Thank you, and you," Rachel replied.

"Hi, I'm Rachel Blackstone," she held out her hand to the man who abruptly stood and shook her hand.

"I'm Tommy Loloma."

Mr. Loloma was a slight but strong man dressed in jeans and a tee, topped with a leather jacket. Rachel's background research revealed he had been formally trained in ballet and modern dance in New York City, but had returned to his native home to perform Hopi ceremonial productions. His hair was shoulder length brunette with a silver streak on one side that ran from his forehead down to his back. He had soft brown eyes and moved with practiced grace of performers. Most troupes are required to take yoga and strength training in addition to dance classes. That made them powerful and elegant.

"Very nice to meet you. Please be comfortable," Rachel said and sat down at the table.

"We've been wondering with all that's going on if we should cancel the festival," Octavia said.

"Oh gosh," Rachel said. "I hadn't thought of that. Personally, I've been trying to keep to my regular schedule." If only they knew. "You're already here and everything is a go for the festival. Your dancers and regalia are here?"

"Yes they are," Octavia replied. "What do you think Tommy?"

"I'm with Rachel. We're all here. Maybe the festival would take people's minds off the scary news stories. I'm good to go if you are. And my dancers are as well."

Octavia hesitated a few seconds.

"Okay," she said. "Let's go ahead as if nothing is amiss."

Like the world ending, Rachel thought but instead said, "Great."

"Tommy, what will you be dancing?"

"The Saquasohuh or Blue Star Kachina."

Rachel gasped.

"Really?" A chill ran down her back. She remembered the words of Másaw when he warned that the mask should not be removed. *If the Blue Star dances and removes his mask the Fifth World begins*. It had been punctuated by the fearsome persona of the Skeleton Man himself.

"Yes, it was the planned dance from the start," he said. "Do you think we should change?"

"Uh no, but it is surprising all things considered."

"There will be one change," he continued. "I will not be removing the mask at the end of the dance ... because of the, uh, current situation. We take it very seriously and don't want to tempt fate."

"That's reassuring," Rachel said. She would not say how relieved she was. Many people wouldn't even know what dance was being recreated in the Plaza, only that it was beautiful.

Rachel heard her tape recorder click as it came to the end on one side. She quickly flipped it over and restarted it, while continuing to take notes. It was an annoying reality to doing interviews. While she preferred a 20-30 minutes appointment, some ran over.

"Is there anything else you would like to add?" Rachel asked. "We did a pretty thorough preview, but this will go into our update file on the website later today."

"Just come," Octavia said. "We know that everyone is concerned about current events, but this is an opportunity to step away from that and experience the beauty of our southwestern Native American dances."

"Well said," Rachel replied. "Thank you both for dropping by our office to do this."

"You're welcome Rachel," Octavia said. "We appreciate your coverage over the years."

"Happy to do it," Rachel said.

They got up to leave, but Rachel couldn't help but say, "Tommy, you will keep that mask on?" She tried to smile, but it felt wrong on her face.

"Yes ma'am," he said. His smile was wonderful on his face. Rachel couldn't help but warm to him. Dancers had always been some of her favorite artists.

She watched them say goodbye to Stella and leave by the front door. Rachel went to her office to write the short interview and post it on their website. As she closed her laptop, she thought it was time to make a prayer stick or pahos. She pulled off paper from a note pad and wrote the words of a Hopi prophecy: "We are all flowers in the Great Spirit's garden. We share a common root, and the root is Mother Earth." It wasn't exactly a prayer but it seemed appropriate.

After wrapping it around a twig, she pulled a box from a bottom drawer. The box held yarn in the four colors of man: red, black, yellow and white. She cut them all the same length. Taking all the strands at once, she carefully twisted the yarn to cover both the note and twig. The remaining strand she tied to make a small loop so it could be hung in a tree.

Rachel stopped by Julian's office before leaving.

"Hi Jules," she said.

"Hi Rach. What's up?"

"If, uh, things don't go well," Rachel stammered. "You've been a great friend and I've loved working here."

Rachel wiped at the corner of one eye. She would not cry. Dammit, she wouldn't.

"We're close then?" Jules asked.

"Yeah," Rachel replied. "I think it will all be over by the end of the weekend; or not. I'm trying to hold out hope."

"But you uncovered the water poaching," he said. "Why didn't that end it?"

"The word is there is someone who is the ringleader. I have to find him, or her, I guess it could be a woman."

"And you're not sure you can?" Jules asked.

"No." Rachel felt defeated at that moment.

"Rachel," Jules began. "When you first began working with me, you know in the beginning years of the magazine."

"Yeah."

"I knew you'd be an excellent reporter," Julian said. "And I anticipated our relationship, both working and friendship, would last as long as we did. Even if the world is all over, I got my wish." Rachel could see his eyes brimming.

"It's okay," Rachel said. "I feel the same. You don't have to say anything more."

"Just this," Julian added. "You always give it your all, regardless."

"Thanks Jules," Rachel added. "I'm going home now. See you Monday."

"See you Monday," Julian said. "Bright and early. No excuses."

Rachel fled before she snot-cried right there.

As she passed Stella's desk, she paused.

"You don't have to say it," Stella said. "Everyone kind of feels it and no one will blame you if things go in a bad way."

"Thanks, Stella, but I will blame me."

Stella walked around her desk and hugged Rachel hard.

"I love you Rachel," Stella said. "Always have."

"I love you back," Rachel said and fled again. She wasn't good at this mushy stuff.

On her way out of the office, she hung the pahos on a tree in the courtyard. It was hung outside so the prayer would constantly rise to the Upper Beings. Although not religious, she nevertheless crossed herself because surely the world needed every chance it could get.

She often thought of Randy, the hero in the small town of Fort Repose, Florida. Pat Frank had created him in *Alas, Babylon* a post apocalyptic story published in 1959. She had been rereading it again lately. Its central theme wasn't so much the remnants of a nuclear attack, but how a small group of people discovered what their strengths were and how they could help established a new, if very different world. Sometimes she thought of how Randy must have felt in the face of the "thousand-year night." Today, she had some idea. Would she have the strength to stop this before it was too late?

CHAPTER 37

Chloe was throwing a small dinner party tonight either to celebrate their friendship or the end of the world. She was convinced that Chloe didn't know which but felt like they should do something. Rachel wanted to pick up a nice bottle of wine for the occasion. She stopped at a liquor store near downtown and ran smack into her brother Chris at the entrance.

"Excuse me," he said not looking up.

"You don't write, you don't call and then you nearly run me down?" Rachel said.

He stopped and the bottles he was carrying clinked together inside the bag.

"What do you want from me?" Chris replied in his best I'm-too-tired-for-this voice. "I'm not going to be here long, so what's the point?"

"You're leaving?" Rachel asked. "You're not staying in Santa Fe?"

"I've got no house, no wife, no kids. I'm living out of a rental car. So I'm going where the job is."

"Where's the job?" Rachel asked.

He looked bad: thin, pale and haunted. Even a short term in prison was life altering.

"Near Carlsbad," he said.

"That's practically the Mexico border," Rachel said.

"Still know your geography," Chris said sarcastically.

Rachel did in fact know her geography. Carlsbad was next to Lea County where the fracking was being done with stolen water. She couldn't help but wonder what this new job entailed.

"You were seen leaving the mining office downtown," Rachel said. "Are you into mining endeavors now? There's fracking going on in that part of the state."

"I'm into eating and took the first job offered me. I'm a felon now, no thanks to you," Chris spit it out his tone full of anger.

"I was only a small part of your arrest. You did the crime. Your decision," Rachel defended herself. "I did save your life."

"So you say," Chris replied. "I was passed out at the time."

He was right. On that stormy night at Tent Rocks as the evil spirit Mario raged, Rachel had to drag Chris to safety he was so exhausted from being held captive. She doubted he cared at the time if he lived or died, but she had. Chris had been involved with Mario and his illegal dealings. Chris went to prison for his part. Mario paid the price with his life.

"You got anything to do with this?" Chris pointed to the Dog Star still spiraling toward a landing on terra firma.

"I was about to ask you the same thing," Rachel said. "It has something to do with water plundering. Knowing about mining would be of prime help to those doing it."

"Well, don't that beat all to hell?" Chris retorted. "Paid my debt to society and already being accused of a new crime."

"Chris, I don't have time to beat around the bush and ask you with hearts and flowers. The world is going to end if this mystery isn't solved."

"Might have known you'd be involved," he said with disgust. "Fooling around with the supernatural stuff is pure idiocy. That Chloe has always been a bad influence."

"We're trying to stop it," Rachel said ignoring the stab at her best friend.

"We're?"

"Chloe and I," she replied. "And others."

"You've become a real ghost buster haven't you," Chris smirked slyly.

"It's a bit more involved than that," Rachel said trying not to rise to the bait.

"Well then, no need to patch things up. The two of you will fuck it up for sure. None of us will be around much longer. Nice to have run into you." Chris pushed the door open.

"I do wish you good luck," Rachel said and meant it.

"Yeah, thanks." Chris walked out of her life, again.

Rachel had grown accustom to his fits of anger and self-righteous resentment. Addictive personalities were frequently incapable of having long-term relationships even if they had given up the addiction. He was forced to give up drinking in prison, but since she saw him in a liquor store with a sack of the hard stuff, she assumed he was making up for lost time. It made her sad, but their family bond or lack thereof was irrelevant at the moment. She watched him drive off in a white Corolla and wondered if she'd ever see him again. Sometimes endings happen and you don't realize it until much later.

* * *

That evening Rachel, Chloe, Dominic, Chile Pod and Juan gathered at Chloe's for dinner. Chloe had outdone herself and the bounty of food and drink on her table would normally have been for a celebration. Instead, it might be goodbye. They ate, drank and laughed at everything. Even Chile Pod and Juan were getting along—unless Juan got too close to Chile's food, then there was a loud discussion that ended with Juan on the other side of the room whining.

Dominic took a last gulp of the wine Rachel had purchased.

"Time for us to go," he said and stood wearily. "We three are the very few who know what is really going on; three neophytes trying to save the world. You two rock. Don't give up until the last second before that bastard star literally blows our world apart. If you need me, I'll be home with Juan tomorrow." He tucked Juan gently into his carrier.

Rachel and Chloe each hugged Dominic in turn. And smooched Juan's head before the carrier door closed.

"And remember," he said. "It's trite, but it isn't over until it's over. 'Night." He topped his head with a driver's cap and left in a whiff of evening air.

Back at the table, Rachel and Chloe clinked glasses.

"Here's to Monday being an ordinary day," Chloe said.

"To ordinary days," Rachel said.

"Do you want to leave Chile Pod in the safe room tomorrow while we're at the festival?" Chloe asked.

"You know, I think she'd be happiest on my bed among all those pillows you love to pile high," Rachel tried to say lightly.

"The ones you throw across the room?"

"I don't just throw them," Rachel retorted. "I'm trying to knock that photo off the dresser. You know the one of me when I was about five years old that Dad gave you."

"You never have liked that photo. And it's so cute."

"I'm holding a fishing pole for heaven's sake," Rachel replied. "I look like the damn dork of the month."

"I'll get extra food and water for Chile Pod."

"Sounds good," Rachel humored her friend. Food and water would be useless in the event of a world-ending catastrophe, but it made Chloe feel better.

"So what do we do?" Chloe asked. "Just go to the festival tomorrow like we would any other day, but keep our eyes open?"

"Yup," Rachel said. "It's what we do."

Rachel showered the best she could with the high-tech shower Chloe had installed she thought just to vex her. After brushing her teeth, she curled up with Chile Pod on the big bed in the suite that Chloe had designed for Rachel and her cat. She tried watching some television, but everything was about the Dog Star and its probable planet-ending descent. Even the talking heads were looking panicked.

Outside on her terrace, she held Chile Pod in her lap and looked up at the other stars. In Santa Fe, there is enough darkness that the stars of the Milky Way can be seen and appreciated. Rachel looked away from Sirius and took a few moments to be grateful for the beautiful night. She noticed the odor of piñon in the air; something she often took for granted. Everything was perfect for that moment. And really, perfection lies in moments.

Rachel went back inside, tucked Chile Pod under the covers letting her head rest lightly on a pillow and curled in around the tiny cat. She took solace in the soft purrs of her companion and the deep quiet of the night. She pretended it was no different from any other.

Chloe had given up trying to sleep too. Instead, she picked up a shawl and her special box of marijuana. She chose a joint, lit it and walked to her terrace where she was surrounded by flowers her gardener had potted for her. He had planted everything in pansies and greenery perfect for autumn. An adobe wall provided privacy but was low enough to see over the top. Tonight, the sky was what she wanted to see. She took a hit and waited for the magic.

She didn't know how or if it was even likely that she and Rachel could find the person behind the ravaging of the aquifer. He or she must be ruthless and have a total disregard for the planet they all called home.

For the moment, she mindfully enjoyed the beauty of the Santa Fe night; the sweeping stars above and the majesty of the rugged mountains. Whatever came next couldn't be much better than this.

Across the city, Julian and Stella sat quietly on the rooftop of the High Desert Country magazine offices looking at the stars and sipping wine. Julian let everyone go home early and wished them a good weekend. Everyone knew he was whistling in the dark. He and Stella stayed. They had known one another from the tough early years of the publication and had great affection for each other.

The evening was cool. They wrapped up in blankets kept for that purpose. If they had to go, this was where they chose to be. Julian covered Stella's hand on the chair arm and she squeezed back gently. They had no words for this moment, only each other's presence.

On the west side, Dominic sat in front of his French doors in the dining room, with his books shelved carefully behind him. He used the room as his office and had a comfortable leather chair for reading. He placed his feet on the hassock and patted his leg for Juan to come up.

Normally, Juan wasn't all that affectionate. Tonight he sensed something up; he complied.

With a small bucket of beers on ice next to him, he opened one and took a sip. What does one do on the last night of the world? Dominic couldn't answer that so he sat with his best friend and a cold one. Maybe he would fall asleep.

Mari-Lynn and Celeste opted to sit within their newly constructed medicine wheel on their property in Tesuque. They had selected it because it had a clearing with a view of the mountains, but also ample trees. They were swathed in one of Mari-Lynn's shawls sitting on meditation cushions. Mari-Lynn had been getting visions all day of the Dog Star crashing. It was unnerving.

Celeste had chosen to change her name when they married. Mari-Lynn thought it perfect for her because it reminded her of the crystal celestine which was blue like her eyes. Since then, Celeste always added some blue color to one side of her hair. Mari-Lynn reached for Celeste's hand. With the other she clutched an amulet of lilac kunzite. It would act as a celestial doorway and facilitate enlightenment in the future, whatever that might be. With candles surrounding them, they waited.

CHAPTER 38

Saturday dawned warm and sunny. Through her window Rachel could see the menacing Dog Star. It was close and large. Just looking at it made her chest tighten and dread settle in her stomach. She brushed her hair; applied light makeup. They had all survived last night. Once again, she wondered if this was the last day of the world.

She knew that the dancer would not remove the mask in his performance of the Blue Kachina, but what if there was another performance in different city and the dancer actually removed the mask? Even if she could find the leader of the water-poaching criminals, would it be in time? That was too many questions for this early in the morning.

She padded into the kitchen with Chile Pod hurrying ahead to see what delectable food Auntie Chloe had put out for her.

"I gave her the best today," Chloe said. "Good morning, little girl. Hi Rachel. Get any sleep?"

"A little," Rachel said.

"Chloe, have we done everything that we could?"

"I was thinking about that last night," Chloe said. "You said it yourself; we need to be suspicious of everyone and everything. Today at the festival there might be a clue, anything. I came up with a plan. If it doesn't work, then at least we will have had an interesting day."

"What's your plan?" Rachel asked.

"Since you don't have a cell, we're going to use these." Chloe set down a box of walkie-talkies on the counter.

"They're set on channel thirty-five. Push this if you need to talk. They're actually faster to use than a cell. You take one side of the Plaza and I'll take the other. We can communicate and watch carefully for any odd behavior; anyone suspicious at all."

"Okay," Rachel replied. "I like it. If we find nothing, we at least did more than just watch the parade."

"If we have to spend our last day, of, uh, anything," Chloe choked a bit. "I can't think of anyone I'd prefer to spend it with."

"Me either," Rachel said, holding up her index fingers and hooking them together in sign language. "Friends forever." They'd done this many times, but today it seemed all the more relevant.

Chloe embraced her friend quickly because she didn't want them in tears, there was too much to do.

"Okay," Chloe coughed. "First we have a healthy breakfast and then off to the Plaza for the festival; and a bit of sleuthing."

"Agreed." Somehow, Rachel knew her last breakfast on Earth would include blueberries and low-fat yogurt!

* * *

Rachel parked the Merc on Palace several blocks from the Plaza. They'd only walked a short distance when the happy noise of voices and music carried down the street to greet them. It sounded as if many people had decided to get out and have a good day despite the ambiguity of the times. Probably the adults were worried, but wanted their children to have fun in spite of it all.

Chloe's cell rang.

"It's for you Rachel," she said. "Dave Chee, the park ranger."

Rachel wondered what this was about. She hoped no more bodies had been discovered in Bandelier.

"Hello Dave." she said.

"Rachel," he hurried. "Remember I told you my mother has second-sight?"

"Yes."

"Well she had a beaut this morning making breakfast," he said. "She said whatever it is, it will happen today. She saw two women. I took that to be you and your friend Chloe. You were both running in the Santa Fe Plaza. She told me to tell you; run like the wind. I can't emphasize that enough; run as fast as you can."

New alarm enfolded Rachel's body. *It was today*. Today the planet, everyone she loved and those she would never know would die if … if she wasn't fast enough?

"Did she see anything else? Like who or what?"

"No, I'm sorry," he said. "She had no further details.

"Are you okay?" he continued.

"Oh Dave, it's bad," Rachel said. "It has something to do with the Dog Star and the end of the Fourth World of the Hopi."

Dave gasped. "Oh my god, I've heard about this my whole life. Does it have anything to do with the water poaching? Is that why you and Chloe were there?"

"Yes, it is because of the men who did it. We have to find the instigator in order to stop the Dog Star."

"Then you should know I saw two men back at the site. I was too far away to make ID, but I tried to get a look at their faces through binoculars."

"And did you?"

"Sorry no," Dave said. "I was too far away. It is possible one had a beard. Can't be sure."

"It does tell me that at least two of the men are still involved and on the loose. That confirms a message from another source."

"Then the world ends today?" Dave asked. "That's what mother meant by *it's today*?"

"Unless we can stop it," Rachel replied. "We're on our way right now."

"In that case, I'll go spend the day with my mother," he said. "I know she'll light a candle. I wish you *bízhánee'*."

"Is that Navajo?" Rachel asked.

"Yes, it means lucky."

"We will need it," Rachel said. "Please thank your mother for me. At least we know that the Plaza is ground zero. That's a great help."

"See you Rachel," he said.

"See you Dave."

Rachel quickly filled in the blanks for Chloe.

"So the Plaza is where we need to be," Chloe said. "I took your advice today and wore shoes I can run in."

"Always good policy," Rachel said, but she couldn't quite manage a smile.

The festival was well attended, all things considered. Although most visitors to the city had gone home because of the generalized panic that existed, there were a few plucky tourists in the Plaza with their cell phones, white athletic shoes and T-shirts with logos or inappropriate sayings.

Throngs of locals who must have decided to defy the circumstances were browsing the arts and crafts tents in the centre of the Plaza while waiting on the Native dances to begin. Booths were set up all over the park and hundreds of people strolled around looking at the paintings, jewelry and myriad of other items. Some were wearing surgical masks. But many were not, preferring to eat instead. The carnita stand was doing a booming business as was the street taco truck despite the hostile proximity of the whirling star.

"Here's your walkie-talkie," Chloe said pulling one from her purse. "I'll take the south side of the Plaza. You stay here on the north side."

Rachel took the walkie-talkie.

"Press here to talk?" She already knew, but wanted Chloe's confirmation.

"Yes," Chloe said. "Oh Rachel, do be careful." She hugged Rachel tightly, and then stood back. "Best friend on the planet."

"Absolute best," Rachel agreed. "Whatever happens, we go down fighting like Butch and Sundance or even better; we win."

"I'll buy the margaritas at The Shed!" Chloe tried to be brave, but Rachel barely saw the tears in Chloe's eyes for those in hers.

"I'm holding you ... to ... that," Rachel choked a bit. She blinked and Chloe was gone into the crowd.

Rachel tried to regain her composure while looking in the store window. There was a display of kachina dolls artistically arranged among miniature straw bales in the window. Her eyes were compelled to look at the Blue Kachina. Something nagged at the cobwebs of her mind. What was it Anna had said? Was it cats-ee-nah?

"Damn!" Realization flooded her with fear and relief. Maybe they did have a chance. Anna meant kahts-ee-nah. It was the Hopi pronunciation of kachina. "Oh geez!"

Now she knew what they had to watch. But why? Tommy was not going to remove the mask. Was Anna wrong? Was Joseph? Yet Anna had repeated it several times. She was certain it was important.

She pushed the talk button on the walkie-talkie.

"Yes Rachel," Chloe said.

"It's the kachina we have to watch. Remember Anna's warning about the kahts-ee-nah. That's the Hopi pronunciation."

"Oh my god, you're right. And neither of us got that!" Chloe replied.

"Yes," Rachel replied. Despite Tommy's promise not to remove the mask, something is up. We can't take our eyes off Tommy."

"Where are you?"

"On San Francisco," Chloe said. "I'll keep a close watch. They've finished staging. They're about to begin."

"Okay," Rachel said.

There was no time to think. The music started and the Blue Star dance was beginning. The Hopi dancers moved into the Plaza via San Francisco Street led by Tommy Loloma in beautiful regalia. The upper portion of his chest was tinted blue. His arms were adorned in blue and white feathers which represented wings. But it was the blue mask that Rachel couldn't stop looking at. Colorful feathers of red, tan and white fanned out on the top and others hung down from the sides. It was stunning to behold.

Something didn't seem right. Tommy was a trained dancer and yet his port de bras or arm carriage, which should have been graceful and full of emotion, were more aggressive than she expected. She watched as he stomped and bowed while the dancers following him seemed to be more composed and fluid. The company chanted in Hopi with each choreographed step.

By this time they were coming around the first corner of the Plaza. People filled every available piece of ground, sidewalk and bench trying to glimpse the pageantry. Even most of the vendors had stopped selling and were watching.

***

Chloe waited until the kachina dancers passed and began to make her way through the street to join Rachel on the other side. Her peripheral vision caught motion in an alley. She went to investigate. Everything and everyone was under suspicion.

This was a famous alleyway because spies had met there to plot the assassination of Trotsky while the leader was living in exile in Mexico City. The Häagen-Dazs ice cream shop was once the location of Zook's Drugstore. It had provided safe haven for Russian spies in and around 1941. It didn't hurt that Zook's had a back door; making for a quick escape for an undercover agent.

The alley was narrow and dark, littered with a couple of Dumpsters. Something blue stirred on the dirty pavement. Chloe ran. There, next to a garbage container she found a man with his chest painted blue.

"Are you all right?" she reached out to take his hand.

He sat up rubbing his head.

"What happened?" Chloe asked.

"I was on my way to perform when I was hit from behind." He continued to massage his head.

"Let me look," Chloe said and carefully parted his hair to find an ugly red bump on his head. A little blood oozed from the wound.

"You've got some swelling," she said. "Does your head hurt?"

"Oh yeah!"

"Let's see if you can stand?" Chloe helped him to his feet while he gripped the Dumpster with one hand to steady himself.

"Well?" Chloe inquired.

"I'll live," he said. "But I'm supposed to be performing. I need to get to my dance company."

"By the way," Chloe asked. "What are you performing?"

"The Blue Star Kachina," he said.

"Oh my god!"

* * *

Rachel tried to position herself where she could see the Hopi troupe as they rounded the last corner and still be in place to witness the end of the dance as they reached the intersection of Palace and Lincoln. She wanted to have as many dancers in sight as possible. Rachel worked her way through the crowd until she reached the top step in front of the art museum. It was a perfect watchtower if no one taller stepped in front of her. With others also jockeying for places, it was easier said than done.

"Rachel, Rachel. Come in," Chloe yelled into the walkie-talkie.

"Here Chloe. What's up?"

"I found your dancer lying in the spy alley," Chloe said. "Someone hit him over the head."

"What?" Rachel yelled. "I can't hear you. What about an alley?"

"I found the Blue Kachina lead dancer passed out in the alley behind the Häagen-Dazs," Chloe replied.

"The spy alley?" Rachel asked.

"That's what I said." Exasperated. "Your dancer is here with me."

"Tommy?"Rachel asked.

Rachel listened as Chloe asked him if he was Tommy.

"Yes Rachel," Chloe's voice squawked. "His name is Tommy Loloma."

"So the guy I'm watching isn't Tommy?" Rachel exclaimed.

"No," Chloe replied.

"Thanks. I've got to get closer," Rachel said.

"I'm on my way to help you," Chloe shouted over the music and cheering of the crowd.

"Will you be okay?" Chloe asked Tommy. "Do you have friends I can leave you with?"

"I'm fine." he said. "My artistic director is here." He pointed to an anxious looking man trying to see his company perform.

"He must not remove the mask," Tommy said. "Stop him at any cost!"

But Chloe had already joined the mass of people all straining for a glimpse of the performance.

* * *

Rachel threaded her way through the people congregating on the museum steps. Before she could reach the street the wind had picked up significantly. She couldn't remember a report saying a weather system was coming through. In fact, she distinctly remembered a sunny calm forecast. Still, the mountain winds could materialize without warning. Vendors were beginning to collect their wares as some pictures and jewelry had fallen with the gusts.

The dancers kept coming along but some had to hold their headdresses in place with one hand as they continued.

Rachel worked her way through the crowd. She was walking head-on into people who were leaving, making it all the more difficult to get to the open street. It seemed imperative that she be in the open. Someone bumped her and she looked up. Not all were going home because of the blustery conditions. The Dog Star was not only perilously close, but it seemed to be what was causing the wind. Rachel could see the commotion on the surface of the star. It too had wind whirling and fires that seemed to belch from holes in the ground. She stopped and stared.

The star was entering the Earth's gravitational pull. Because it was so close, the fires appearing on the surface were apparent to the eye. Parts of the star were burning as it entered the atmosphere.

* * *

Chloe was making her way to the other side of the Plaza where the dance would end. The wind had become so strong that many vendors were trying to dismantle their tents. Two had blown away. The remnants of one flapped from the roof of the Palace. The festival flags hanging from the Palace were taking a beating too with a few missing in action.

A little girl fell in front of her.

"Are you okay?" she asked.

The girl nodded her head, but she was obviously afraid.

"I can't find my mom," she said.

"Okay sweetie," Chloe said. "I'm going to pick you up and we'll look for your mother."

It was enough. A worried young woman came running through the mass of people, shoving where necessary. She scooped her off Chloe's shoulder.

"Thank you. Thank you," she said.

"I'm just glad you were close by." She smiled at the girl. "You're okay now."

Chloe looked around for Rachel and saw her emerging from the spectators on the other side. Reaching her would be a trick. The TV crew was blocking the way with their truck. Oddly, they seemed to be filming something behind her instead of the dancing. Chloe turned and looked behind her. There were more people. Another company of dancers was marching into the Plaza. Except for the awful wind, everything seemed normal, until she glanced upward, above the park, the people, the buildings and saw something so horrifying she wanted to look away but couldn't.

CHAPTER 39

Rachel finally disentangled herself from people and stood behind one of the street barriers. The wind was so angry. It was the worst red flag warning ever. Several dancers were still performing in the best *the show must go on* tradition. Some thought better of it and dropped out to take cover from flying objects. Others wore frightened faces and kept looking south. No sky appeared in that direction, only a mass of hurtling rock.

Chloe squeezed from behind the TV truck, and looped her purse over one shoulder and across her waist so she could move freely.

The walkie-talkie barked: “In place Rachel.”

“I see you,” Rachel answered. “Good luck friend.” She pocketed the walkie-talkie. Every muscle in her body was screaming with readiness.

The lead dancer came to the end of the street and stopped. Rachel wanted to breathe a sigh of relief, but she knew he wasn’t Tommy. The lack of a silver stripe in his hair confirmed that. What was he going to do? He didn’t knock Tommy on the head for no reason.

With a flourish, he reached up to remove the mask.

“Oh no!” Rachel yelled. “No you don’t!”

Chloe saw him at the same time. She took off from her place in front of the bank.

Rachel was already running. Dave Chee’s words echoed in her head. “Run like the wind.”

She gave it all she had, pumping her arms and legs. Her hair billowed behind her.

The dancer wasn't yet aware that anyone was close to him because the mask wrapped around his face obstructing his peripheral vision. He was either unfamiliar with the mask or wanting to make a grand flourish.

Before Rachel could reach him, the shaking started. It was so intense she feared it would be impossible to move forward. The quake caught the dancer off guard. He averted his eyes from the frightened spectators as the street trembled beneath his feet.

Rachel slowed down, but she was still making headway. The ground felt strange as each foot came in contact. She had to really focus on placement of her feet or she would fall. A few more steps and she could tackle him, but she had to be careful not to knock the mask off. The dance could not be completed.

She battled the wind and the tectonic forces as she planned her attack. Knocking him down could dislodge the mask. It must be finessed. He seemed bewildered by the commotion and kept looking down. Rachel was at last behind him. She did what flight attendants do during an emergency landing when someone won't jump out the door; she punched the back of both knees and he went down.

"Hold the mask on!" Rachel shouted as Chloe arrived.

The two of them pushed him all the way down and held him. Police working the festival showed up.

"What's going on!" one demanded. "Why are you holding this man?"

"He's an imposter," Rachel shouted above all the noise.

"Someone stop the music!" Chloe said. "The music must stop! Do you fucking hear me!" she yelled.

She must have used her authoritative voice because one of the cops obediently ran to the bandstand where the orchestra still played.

A few seconds later, the music ended, the seismic activity ceased and wind stopped. It was as if they were in the eye of a hurricane.

"Make sure no one is dancing," Rachel said.

"Just a minute," one of the cops said. "Who do you think you are?"

"Please," Rachel said. "This man is an imposter and may be a criminal. We can't remove the mask until the festival is at full stop."

"That's nuts!" he said.

"Humor me, okay?" Rachel was afraid. Afraid it would all be for nothing.

The man squirmed beneath them.

"Let me up!" he demanded. His voice sounded familiar, but Rachel couldn't place it.

An officer nodded to his underling signaling from the bandstand.

"Okay, everything is stopped. Now what's going on?"

"Do you think it's okay?" Chloe asked.

"Can't be certain," Rachel replied. "I think so."

The officer rolled the man over. He carefully removed the mask and a long black wig.

Rachel gasped. "Dr. Saxon!"

CHAPTER 40

"What the hell?" Rachel said.

"This is Dr. Axel Saxon from the UNM." She informed the police.

"We'll sort it out at the station," an officer said. "You're all under arrest."

"What? No!" Chloe said.

"This is the man who is responsible for the water poaching near Bandelier," Rachel said.

"We thought we could control it," Saxon admitted. "No one was supposed to get hurt."

"Don't know what you're talking about," The officer replied. "This looks like assault to me; the two of you knocking him down. You can tell your story at the station."

He moved to take her arm. Rachel heard cuffs jingle in his hand. Before he could lock them around her wrists, the wind intensified again; this time from the other direction.

"What the hell is with the wind?" the policeman asked.

Before anyone could contemplate that question, people and anything not attached scooted along the ground. Parents grabbed their children's hands and clutched onto trees in the usually peaceful park. Those who could went inside stores. Every window on the Plaza had a face pressed up against it from inside.

A wolf's call rang out cutting through the pandemonium. Rachel tugged on Chloe's arm.

"That's our cue," Rachel said.

They made tracks while the officers tried to help others. Rachel saw them push Saxon into the patrol car. They were so busy rounding up small children they had no time to look for two women disappearing into the human swarm. The women raced to the east side of the Plaza.

"What's going on Rachel?" Chloe asked.

"Look at the Dog Star," Rachel answered. "Do you think it's moving away?"

"Damn Rachel, you may be right."

"It's sucking at the Earth as it reverses direction," Rachel said.

Dust from the mountains north of the city began blowing through downtown. The flags atop the art museum were unfurled southward. Parents took off jackets and placed them over their kids' heads. Not everyone could get inside as the stores had filled with festival refugees. Those with surgical masks whipped them out. Between the dust storm and flying objects, it was difficult to breathe or move. For the moment, chaos reigned.

"Come on," Chloe yelled to be heard. "Inside La Fonda."

They crossed the street bumping into others as they made slow progress. Inside the lobby, it was a madhouse. People cried openly in fear and asked repeatedly, "What's happening?"

"Let's go to the roof," Rachel said.

When the elevator opened on the fifth floor, there was no one in the anteroom that accessed the rooftop bar. From where they stood, they could see outside through French doors. There were no takers today. Several of the chairs had fallen over on the decking. Glasses were smashed and littered the floor. Someone would have to clean up the mess—if anyone survived.

The huge Dog Star strained against the Earth's gravity. It needed to gain momentum to make its retreat, but it was having a hard time.

"I think we did it Rachel!" Chloe said excited. "It looks like it's trying to move away."

"Is it so close that it can't let go?" Rachel asked.

The surface of Sirius churned with stardust as fires flickered and became infernos. From inside their protected lookout they could see the tentativeness of the star as it tried to pull back and at the same time was held by gravity.

"Rachel, are we too late?" Chloe asked.

"I don't know. That's the trouble with this mystical stuff. I'm only a cog in a very large wheel. There are more powerful forces at work."

"If it doesn't get unstuck, I'm afraid we're going to be losing buildings instead of just windows," Chloe yelled above the din. "Could it suck all of us out there with it?"

"I'm going to call on Joseph and see if he can assist us," Rachel said.

I hear you. Rachel heard the words even though they were not spoken aloud. *Ring the bell.*

"Bell?" she said aloud while Chloe watched her friend as she communicated with the spirit world. "Joseph, do you mean the bell here on the rooftop?"

Yes, ring the bell.

"We have to ring the bell," Rachel said. "Come on. Careful of the broken glass."

"But Rachel, I can only remember a chandelier. Is there a bell in the tower?"

Rachel got closer minding the broken glass; she looked up into the bell tower.

"There seems to be a bell today," Rachel observed.

"Then we ring that bastard!" Chloe exclaimed.

Between the glass and the windstorm it was a major effort to reach the tower. Metal chairs were sliding across the rooftop and crashing into the walls that surrounded the bar. When they reached the tower; there was a bell and pull.

"Wait Rachel, what was the other thing Anna said?"

"The thing about the powder? Oh my god, not powder, power! Let the power go through you. Joseph has told me this before. Feel it!"

"How?" Chloe asked.

"Pretend you're meditating," Rachel shouted. "Be open to it, but don't hold onto it."

"Here," Rachel grasped the rope. "Let's both take the rope and ring this thing."

For several minutes the women pulled the rope over and over, sometimes leaving the floor in the effort. Rachel once again sensed the spiritual power rushing through her body. She remembered to let it go, not to hold onto it.

And then the spiritual force she felt changed to something else. It was similar to the low atmospheric pressure drop prior to an approaching storm.

"Wait," Rachel said. "Did you feel the pressure change?"

"Yes!" Chloe said and looked at the Dog Star. "Oh god, Rachel. It's happening."

Together they rang the bell until the wind stopped. They stepped back and watched the sky.

When it seemed the star was making its return flight to the heavens, they stood, sweaty, exhausted from exertion.

As they watched, Sirius headed homeward first leaving the Earthly bonds with a fiery burst and then slowly backing away like a dancer who gracefully moves to the back of the stage and disappears behind the curtain. Poof!

"Rachel!" Chloe embraced her friend. "We did it!"

They jumped up and down like they did as little girls screaming with joy.

"It appears we have," Rachel wiped at her eyes, but Chloe's eyes streamed with tears.

"I've never been so frightened in my life," Chloe said.

"That makes two of us," Rachel said. "You were great. I couldn't have done it without you."

"You would have found a way," Chloe replied.

"No, seriously, Chloe. Thank you.

"And you owe me a margarita," Rachel said gruffly, not wanting to give in to her emotions.

"Let's see if we can wobble over to The Shed," Chloe replied. "It will be heaven."

"It's going to take more than one," Rachel held the door for Chloe and punched the elevator button.

"Oh, I'm going to tell the barkeep to line them up!" Chloe said.

Outside, in the southern sky, the Dog Star regained its position as it slowly slipped below the horizon.

The Fourth World of the Hopi would not end today.

They looked at each other and began to laugh. They were alive. And everyone they loved was alive and everyone they would never know was alive.

CHAPTER 41

Rachel sat in her kitchen office corner with Chile Pod on her lap. Typical days are so underrated. We sometimes mistake them for boring. But should a loved one become ill or die, we experience a home break-in or a fender bender, all we want is to feel normal again. So Rachel was enjoying an average day with her tiny companion while finishing stories to meet her deadlines.

Dr. Saxon had been behind the water-poaching scheme. Because of his knowledge of geology, he thought he could control the explosions so as not to cause earthquakes and push the supervolcano to eruption. But he had not entertained starting the countdown to the Hopi Day of Purification. He'd been careless in his hiring practices and several of the men went rogue, killing two of the university's own people. Soon he found himself in over his head and out of control. Rachel believed without supernatural help from Joseph and Kiyiya, she and Chloe would also have perished.

Saxon and his henchmen would be standing trial for several counts including murder, kidnapping, assault, unlawful mining and removal of water. There would likely be charges filed by several of the Northern Pueblo tribes. Rachel didn't think Saxon set out to kill anyone, but the fact remained two people had died for nothing. His motive was the low pay of university professors. Didn't it always boil down to money and greed? Hadn't it always?

Mahatma Gandhi said: *Earth provides enough to satisfy every man's needs, but not every man's greed.* He was chillingly correct.

Many houses and businesses were damaged as a result of the earthquakes and the wind. Elk in the Valles Caldera had succumbed to the deadly fumes the volcano had coughed up. The full scope of the damage to wildlife was yet to be determined, but it was thought that many wild creatures may have died.

Of course, Saxon didn't believe in the Hopi prophecies, but he also couldn't explain why the Dog Star had moved from its place in the cosmos and threatened the Earth and everyone with an Anasazi apocalypse.

The news media was trying to scientifically explain the behavior of Sirius, but were having trouble creating a spin for it. Conspiracy websites were ecstatic with their own theories. They'd be busy talking about all the ramifications for years.

The Hopi tribe remained silent, but Rachel wondered if they spoke knowingly among themselves. They were called the Peaceful Ones, and she didn't expect that would change.

The tremors were tapering off and much less intense. The Valles Caldera in all its majesty was still emitting a little smoke, but it too seemed to be reentering a time of dormancy. There had been no more bird or fish kills and no flooding. Even the wind had not exceeded Santa Fe's customary breezy conditions.

She had kept her promise to be at work the Monday after the day of reckoning; so had everyone else. And while there were brief and quiet conversations about survival and questions about the cause, it seemed most people just wanted to return to their daily lives.

On that Monday, Rachel found a gift from Jules on her desk; a cell phone! It came with a note: "Please keep this with you should you need help. Otherwise, you never have to use it." He had added a smiley face. She tried to take it in the spirit it was given, but eyed it warily.

Mari-Lynn and Celeste were back in their shops conducting business as usual. Thus far, New Mexico hadn't passed recreational marijuana, but there was plenty of demand for the medicinal kind. Mari-Lynn was beginning classes in spirituality and crystal powers. Her shop was a bona fide hit.

Anna was now in a more challenging school for highly intelligent students; with a scholarship. She had reported to Rachel no further visits from the other side. They were forever united in their experiences.

Chris had not put in another appearance nor had she heard from him. Somehow, she didn't think he was gone forever. It was too bad. They had been close growing up, but somewhere he had taken a wrong turn into illegal activities and bad behavior.

Dave Chee's mother had predicted the time and place where the Fifth World of the Hopi would commence if the star wasn't stopped. Rachel would be grateful to her as long as time played out. Seeing Chee again was not at all an unattractive idea. She hoped that could be arranged. Maybe she could meet his mother and learn about her psychic gift.

If she hadn't been there this whole scenario would be difficult to believe. She and Chloe, with the help of some great friends, had stopped the end of the world. But they couldn't tell or explain it to anyone outside of their close-knit circle. No one but her friends and the scientists who studied the Dog Star would ever know how close the inhabitants of the blue planet came to annihilation.

It was still difficult to cope with these paranormal occurrences, but Rachel was grudgingly accepting the fact that these episodes were not going to stop and she might as well do her best to rise to each. She had terrific friends in Chloe, Dominic, Mari-Lynn, Julian and Stella; not just supportive, but ready to take on whatever they could to help.

Having submitted her stories, she popped the cap off a beer and went outside with Chile Pod at her heels. They relaxed under the tree next to the herb bed, which was flourishing in spite of the late planting. Chile Pod curled up on her lap and purred contentedly. The tortie's soft fur and the peaceful evening was more than enough to appreciate for the moment.

Rachel wondered if there would ever come a time when people in their never-ending attempts for more would understand they could not eat money; before they destroyed the only home we would ever have. She'd leave that to the philosophers.

DID YOU ENJOY ANASAZI MEDIUM?

If so, please consider writing a short review for Amazon or Goodreads. Thank you for reading.
G G Collins

Check out the blogs:

https://reluctantmediumatlarge.wordpress.com/
https://paralleluniverseatlarge.wordpress.com/

ABOUT THE AUTHOR

A seasoned reporter, G G Collins has racked up a lot of column inches, a few awards and a university arts fellowship. She learned the ins and outs of publishing at a book publisher.

Working as a reporter is one of the most educational jobs. It's the job of a reporter to ask questions, learn quickly and write even faster about many subjects. In one day, you can cover a fundraiser for COVID-19 research, meet an entertainer in town for a weekend performance and attend a press conference for a local brewery. The next day, it's the new heart center, getting a first grader's take on saving a historical building and welcoming the new sharks at the aquarium.

The result of thousands of interviews, press conferences and performances is that journalists learn a little bit about many things. Alexander Pope wrote, "A little learning is a dangerous thing." He also authored in the same poem: "Fools rush in where angels fear to tread." Both could be applied to reporters, many of whom rush to breaking news sites that could be the location of a terrorist attack, a hurricane landing or a bank robbery.

It's never a dull moment for her protagonist, reporter Rachel Blackstone, who takes more time off to solve paranormal mysteries than she does for vacations.

Bibliography for Further Reading:

Book of the Hopi by Frank Waters
The Fourth World of the Hopis by Harold Courlander
Star Ancestors: Extraterrestrial Contact in the Native American Tradition by Nancy Red Star
Bandelier National Monument
Valles Caldera, Jemez Volcanic Field, New Mexico Museum of Natural History & Science

www.ingramcontent.com/pod-product-compliance
Lightning Source LLC
LaVergne TN
LVHW050630100826
845148LV00011B/1821

* 9 7 8 1 7 3 5 4 2 8 2 0 8 *